This is for Jon.

Acknowledgements:

I am grateful to Debra Hines Thornton, Lynn Cline, Michael Dickey, Phillip Krummrich, Brian White, and Resa Willis for their friendship and encouragement.

I would also like to express my appreciation for the women of my life: my mother, Beatrice, and my two sisters, Lea Anne and Mary Lynne.

And I thankfully acknowledge the Missouri Arts Council for a 1990 Missouri Writers Biennial Grant which enabled me to complete this book.

The cover design is by Michael Dickey.

The
Things
I've Got
Growing
Deep
Down
Inside

Contents

Girls

Will

Be

Girls

Swimming at Flat Bridge, 1963

Mother and Aunt Mel were already tight-lipped because we'd been swimming at Flat Bridge three hours with no sign of the men or even their flat-bottomed river boat. They got tight-lipped when the men went on weekend fishing trips by themselves. It was like they knew those men were having fun without them, probably whizzing off the side of the boat and cussing and looking out for women sunning themselves on the river banks, and Mother and Aunt Mel didn't like it one bit. Only Aunt Wildeen didn't seem to care. She was the youngest, and she had been sunning herself on the banks of the river by Flat Bridge all afternoon, while a few of the Poindexter boys stole glances at her as they paddled by in their underwear. She did look good in a bathing suit. She had on a two-piecer print of yellow flowers with bottoms that came to just below her belly button. Her blond hair was tied up in a red scarf. She was married to Uncle Benny, my dad's youngest brother.

They'd only been married three months. She was from Chicago, and she always kept her hair done up and painted her toenails and wore lipstick so red it was all I could see on her face when she talked to me. She had never been outside of Chicago until she married Benny, and they moved back home. She called herself "Pioneer Wildeen" and said her friends from high school would never believe she could move this far south. She typed letters and mailed them off and got letters back from places like Milwaukee and Toledo. I watched her type once when I was over at their house to bring Uncle Benny my dad's monkey wrench so Benny could work on his bathroom pipes. She typed a whole page in about a minute.

Her name before she got married was Wildeen Wilde. I remember that because I read it on the invitation, and because at the party after the wedding my Uncle Benny who was already drunk before he even stepped up to the altar, took my daddy by the lapels and danced around the room with him saying, "I married a Wilde woman!"

7

I was in the wedding. I threw flower petals on the floor just before Wildeen marched down the aisle in her wedding dress. I was thirteen, and it was the first time I'd ever worn a long dress, and it wasn't bad except for the girdle and nylons, and the lace on my slip which made me break out in a rash.

For some reason Aunt Wildeen liked me from the first time she met me. Uncle Benny had brought Wildeen over for dinner to meet Daddy, and when Benny said, "Oh yeah, and this is Esther," Wildeen came straight over to me and shook my hand.

"You're tall for your age," she said to me.

I nodded and let go of her hand.

"Your hair's too short and could use a perm," she said. She studied my face. "You've got good bone structure though. You'll always be pretty 'cause you've got good bone structure."

Benny thumped me on the head as he walked into the family room where the ball game was going on the TV. "We call her Mudface, for short," he said, and he laughed.

"You will always be Esther to me," said Wildeen. She said the words as if she'd just heard them in some movie and had been waiting for the right moment to use them herself. I liked it though. I liked being included in her drama.

I looked at my mother who was standing nearby. She had a smile on, but it was one of those that didn't show any of her teeth. "Would you like something to drink?" she said to Wildeen. "Iced tea? Lemonade?"

"I'll have whatever the boys are drinking," Wildeen said. And she went straight into the family room, sat down in Daddy's big chair by the TV and said, "Who's playing?"

Aunt Wildeen was Catholic. A priest did their wedding. All through the ceremony the priest and Wildeen and Benny crossed themselves and knelt and said things in Latin. I'd never seen a priest up close before. This one had a fleshy neck that spilled over his collar, and one side of his face was covered with tiny red webs. Daddy said they were capillaries and later at the party while the priest was drinking champagne, I heard him tell someone that years ago he'd been hit in the face with a golf club.

Wildeen's parents didn't come to the wedding because Benny wasn't Catholic even though he promised the priest he would raise his kids Catholic and go through the classes to convert. A few Wilde cousins showed up for the reception though and stole six cases of champagne. I watched one of them named Rudy carry a case out to his trunk and place it next to two other cases. He saw me standing nearby and said, "It's for the honeymoon, kid. We're taking it over to the motel where Wildeen and Buddy are staying to surprise them."

"His name is Benny," I said.

"Oh. Right." He took a crumpled dollar out of his pocket and gave it to me. Then he lit a cigarette, climbed into his Impala, and rolled down the window. "You Catholic?" he said to me, blowing smoke from his mouth and nose.

"No," I said.

He nodded, still looking at me. "I've gone out with girls who weren't Catholic," he said, like he was trying to tell me that there was still hope. He smoked on his cigarette a bit more and stared at his dashboard. Then finally he said, "Well, gotta run." He started the car, and before he drove off he flicked his half-smoked cigarette out the window.

I wiped the butt off on the hem of my dress and finished it. I'd been smoking for a year, in the field behind my house. I hadn't told anybody. It takes a lot of practice to look right smoking, and I wasn't very good at it yet, because cigarettes were hard to come by. I usually had to steal them from my dad or from Aunt Mel when she left her purse open on our kitchen counter and she and Mother were out back clipping fresh flowers or something. On this particular night though, I didn't even hide but stood out in the parking lot in my long pink dress, smoking and hoping someone would catch me, pulling at my girdle which was starting to itch and wondering, since I'd just learned in last year's gym class the facts of life, if Wildeen and Benny had ever done it before or if this night would be their first time.

Aunt Wildeen had that effect upon people. She made people think about physical things. So my mother and Aunt Mel got thin-lipped around her, and Benny was always grabbing her by the hips, and even my dad who never listened to women talk because he said he didn't like the high-pitched sound of their voices—even Dad would smile and watch her lips move as she was speaking. And now, at the river, while crawdads skittered around on the rocks and dragonflies, locked together in twos and threes, lighted on people's wet heads, the Poindexter boys kept swimming past Wildeen and craning their neck's like a bunch of hungry turtles.

"Ess," my mother yelled at me from the bank. I was standing in river water up to the top of my thighs, the water swirling about me, cold and brown from the mud I'd stirred up with my tennis shoes. I didn't especially like swimming, but the sun was too hot for just sitting on the rocks of the banks. I couldn't just lie there motionless, minute after minute like Wildeen did. "Esther!" my mother said again.

9

"What is it?" I answered, without turning back to look at her.

"Don't let Philip go down the river so far! He's heading for the drop off. Mel says he's going to drown."

"I can swim," Philip yelled. He was chucking stones at a log on the far bank, trying to hit a row of turtles sunning themselves, but so far he hadn't come within ten feet.

"No you can't," said Aunt Mel.

Philip was my ten year old cousin, Aunt Mel's only son. I hated him. He liked to pull the legs off of june bugs and pinched hard enough to make blue marks on my arms and was always reaching for my bra strap to snap it when I wasn't looking. His dad kept Philip's hair cut in a tight crewcut, and he had one of those hard boy faces. I had to sit next to him on the hot ride down to the river. I nearly always got car sick and I thought if I did this time, I'd be sure and throw up on Philip since he had been sitting next to me farting and laughing the whole trip.

"Philip," Aunt Mel kept saying, "if you pass gas one more time, I'll slap your face."

I kept wishing she would. Please, oh, please, I'd think. Slap his face. But she never would.

If he was drowning, he wouldn't have let me save him anyway. So, while I waded slowly in the direction of where Philip was swimming, I stayed just far enough away that I wouldn't get there in time.

The Poindexter boys were horsing around on Paralysis Rock. Paralysis Rock was a big clump of rocks if you want to be particular. They jutted over the river and formed a kind of diving platform, but the water was too shallow to go head first so a person had to half jump, with his knees tucked up under his chin and let his rear end hit the bottom first.

The Poindexters had a family plot right next to ours in the church cemetery. In fact, they had the oldest family plot in the church yard, at least that's as far as I could tell from reading all the headstones on Decoration Day while Mother and Aunt Mel placed wreaths and cried over the headstones of Granny and Granpa and Uncle Short and the twins, baby brothers to Mother and Aunt Mel who died at six months of age, one within a day of the other. Besides the twins' grave (it had a single headstone as they were buried together, arm in arm from what Mother tells me when I can get her to talk about it), the oldest Poindexter headstone was my favorite because there was a picture on it of the occupant, Harris Poindexter. His face, somehow transferred to porcelain and embedded in the stone, looked not much older than mine and he had this shocked expression, hair half standing up, eyebrows raised, mouth open . . . like dying had caught him off guard. The gravestone had some dates I can't remember and the words . . . "died too young." And whenever I stood in front of his gravestone I got a creepy feeling all the way down to the heels of my feet that Harris Poindexter was looking back at me. And the way his face looked, something about his eyebrows and his open mouth, made me feel like I owed him an answer to some question I just missed hearing.

I noticed now that all of the boys on the rock had that same kind of look about them, thick dark hair, thick eyebrows that always seemed half raised, except for one that the boys called DeWayne who had sandy colored hair and eyes so close together it looked like someone had squeezed his head together as a baby and it had never popped back out.

Mother didn't care much for the Poindexter boys. Anyone who would swim in his underwear for the whole wide world to see and with ladies present was no better than an animal. She always called them "Those Poindexter Boys."

"Ess," she had said, as we were unloading towels and blankets and the picnic baskets with strawberry soda pops and sandwiches already gummy from the heat, "don't go near those Poindexter boys." She used her low "you know what I mean" voice. The way she looked at me then, with a woman to woman look, made me wonder if by swimming in their thin underwear those Poindexter boys set sperm loose in the murky river water. I'd learned about sperm in gym class too. Mrs. Lee, my leathery gym teacher, had warned us in her high-pitched voice that "sperm could swim upstream in even the swiftest of currents so determined it is to reach its destination!"

Mother didn't warn me about looking at those Poindexter boys though. Mother and Aunt Mel were lying on their stomachs with their faces away from the river and separated from Wildeen by about ten feet. They were propped up on their elbows talking about someone and paying no attention to me. So I waded thigh-high in the water and pretended to study the river bottom for crawdads and watched closely as the Poindexters pushed and shoved one another on Paralysis Rock, the thin skin of their underwear clinging to them and showing the hint of something pink bouncing around just beneath the surface.

DeWayne was wearing boxers and was just about to be shoved over the edge of the rocks to where I might get a good enough view of something to report back to my friend Debra

Jean who took gym class with me and had once said she saw a flasher standing in a second story window of the public library (he had the shade drawn down to about his waist and was tapping at the window as she walked by on the sidewalk below so as to get her attention, but she said it was dark and she hardly saw anything at all) when all of a sudden someone came up behind me and shoved me under the water. I thought it was Philip, the little creep, so before I even came up for a breath, I grabbed his feet and yanked as hard as I could so that he came down in one loud splash, and it was only after I saw the yellow flowered bathing suit that I realized it wasn't Philip at all but Wildeen. I stood up in the water right then and pushed the hair back out of my face and reached for her arm, saying before she even came up out of the water, "I'm sorry, Aunt Wildeen. I thought it was Philip," because I figured she'd be mad at me for getting her hair wet, since most women once they get older don't like to get their hair wet when they are swimming, so they're always doing side strokes, even with their bathing caps on, the way Mother and Aunt Mel do, but when Wildeen came up sputtering and tugging here and there at her suit she was laughing so hard she could barely catch her breath.

"I saw you," she said in her loud voice like she didn't care who heard us, and she didn't, I knew that. "I saw you trying to look up those boys' shorts," she said still laughing.

"I was looking for crawdads," I said just as loud. I could feel my face getting hot, and I wasn't sure if it was from being in the sun and water for three hours or from being mad at getting caught and having to lie about it.

Wildeen pulled the wet red scarf from her pony tail and bent over throwing her hair out ahead of her. Even wet her hair was blond and wavy. She twisted her hair up into a tight rope and wound her red scarf around it again. As she lifted her head to look at me I could see short curls springing up like thin copper wires all over her head where her hair refused to be held in place.

"Well, you won't find any crawdads up there," she said, waving her hand in the direction of the Poindexter boys. "But," then she winked at me, "you might find something else that bites!" She laughed again, and I could feel my face getting hotter. Wildeen said, "Come on," and she swam off in the direction of the drop off.

I looked back at Mother and Aunt Mel. They had their heads down now so it looked like they were sleeping. Like I said, I didn't care for swimming much, and didn't like to get my hair wet because it made my cheek bones look bigger, and it emphasized my pointy chin. But when I saw Wildeen down by the drop off, waving at me, I just dove in and swam straight for her and when I came up out of the water she was still laughing.

"You're the funniest looking swimmer I've ever seen," she said. And I thought of my pointy chin and big cheek bones and how dumb I must've looked. But instead of getting out of the water and going to sit on a towel, I laughed too.

I turned my back on everyone else, on Mother and Aunt Mel and the Poindexter Boys and Philip and laughed as loud as I could. And that's when I understood why Mother and Aunt Mel didn't like Wildeen and why Benny was so crazy about her.

Wildeen dropped back in the water and began backstroking up the current. I was swatting dragonflies away from my shoulders and the hairs on my back stood up as the hot sun dried the water off my back. And that's when Aunt Mel screamed.

It was an awful scream, not real loud but wavering like the last sound of someone being strangled before their air passage is closed off completely.

"Oh, God!" she said. "Philip!" She ran down to the river's edge. "Esther! Where's Philip?"

Mother was off her towel, too. I turned around to the log where the turtles had been sunning. There were only two left, and I watched as one slid into the water and swam further downstream.

Aunt Mel started into the water, her arms waving about and her crying out, "Philip! Baby!"

Wildeen was standing in the water now. She yelled to Mother to keep Mel out of the water. She'd muddy it up to where we couldn't see. And I remembered hearing Benny brag about how Wildeen had taken life saving classes at the Y in Chicago and how as part of her test she had to jump in the deep water with all her clothes and keep her head above water for nearly twenty minutes.

"Where'd you last see him?" Wildeen said to me.

At first I couldn't even answer. I couldn't even remember. But Wildeen yelled at me. *"Where'd you last see him!"*

"At the edge of the drop off," I said, pointing. "He was by that tree, throwing rocks at the turtles."

She swam in that direction, then stood up, and moving slowly, hunched over, she swept her arms through the muddy water. "Get some help," she said to me. "Get those boys."

I turned in the direction of Paralysis Rock. I could see the boys just beyond the bluff and yelled at them. But they didn't hear over the sound of the river and their own horsing around. A few years back a four-year-old girl had drowned in the river. Down by Eddyville. She floated eight miles and then got caught up under the bridge. Daddy was in on that search and I remembered him telling Mother about how when they found the girl, the searchers were pulling the body along the river by its feet, and he said it was awful the way they let her head bounce against the rocks. But then when the reporters got there, the searchers were real careful with how they handled the body.

I yelled again, this time so loud it made my ears ring. And DeWayne, the one with the close eyes, came to the edge of the rock. "My cousin—we lost him. I think he's drowning somewhere," I said.

DeWayne said something to the other boys, and they all jumped off the rock together, and I pointed them in the direction of Wildeen, and they thrashed and splashed their way over to her.

She yelled at them, just like she yelled at Aunt Mel. To keep back and not thrash around. She told them to form a line and walk forward waving their arms like this, she said, and she showed them. Once they got to the drop off, they'd try diving. And they did just what she said and everyone got real quiet so that the only sound was the water rushing around us and Aunt Mel whimpering on the shore.

I started thinking about how it would change everybody's life, with Philip drowning. Aunt Mel would never get over it, and I was starting to feel sorry about the whole mess, when Philip walked out of the woods down near the log where I last saw him, the little creep.

"What's going on?" he said.

"Philip!" Aunt Mel wailed. She ran across the shore and threw her arms around him. Then she stood back and slapped his face.

"Ow!" Philip said.

"Don't ever do that again," she said. And she started hitting him again. She kept hitting him and hitting him until he ran from her and even then she chased after him waving her arms to try and hit him some more.

"I just had to pee!" Philip kept saying.

"I thought you were dead! Do you realize that, young man?" she wailed. And Mother was chasing after Mel saying, "It's alright. Everything's alright!"

Philip ran for the station wagon, jumped in and locked all the doors before Aunt Mel could reach him and hit him again.

14

The Poindexter boys were laughing. DeWayne looked right at me and winked.

I could hear Aunt Mel yelling at Philip to unlock the doors and him saying through the rolled up windows, "Not until you promise to stop hitting me!"

I looked at Wildeen then. She was standing in the water, watching Aunt Mel and Philip and Mother, not smiling or frowning or anything. Just watching. And I wondered what she was thinking. Something in the way she was standing told me that one way or another, with Benny or without, Wildeen wasn't going to be around here for much longer.

"Esther!" Mother yelled. "Get your things. We're leaving. The boys can just hitchhike home, for all I care."

She was gathering up the towels as she spoke, shaking the rocks from them.

But I pretended not to hear, and dove into the water, swimming toward Wildeen and the edge of the drop off.

Everyday Living

Ruby sat up in bed and held her eyelids open with her fingers until she was awake. The room was dark and still. The space next to her was empty; the spread untouched.

Ruby got out of bed and pulled on her robe. She tied the belt in a knot, drew the collar up around her neck, and started down the hall.

She could hear the TV going. She saw the grey light of the set flickering against the wall before she saw Cyrus stretched out on the couch, snoring like a bullfrog. There was a black and white comedy on—"I Love Lucy," where Lucy has a job dipping frozen bananas in chocolate sauce and rolling them in nuts.

Cyrus' mouth was open and his jaw was sagging the way a dead person's might if it wasn't sewn shut. He had his hands folded across his stomach.

"Why don't you sleep on a bed? That's what they're for."

She said this aloud, but she could have said it to herself. Cyrus didn't so much as twitch.

Ruby rubbed her backside and yawned. "You'll get arthritis if you keep sleeping on the couch. Every couch dozer I've ever known came down with arthritis before they were sixty. My uncle's joints got so inflamed they swole up like apples."

Ruby walked behind the couch so she could see both the TV and Cyrus. "Or cancer maybe. You might get cancer," she said.

On the TV, a man was showing Lucy how to do her job. He took a tray of bananas from a freezer. They were all laid out, each with a wooden stick in one end, the bananas steaming with cold. He showed her how to load up a machine with bananas so they came rolling out on a conveyer belt one by one. He showed her how to dip them in a vat of melted chocolate at the end of the belt, roll them in nuts, then stand them up by their wooden sticks in a tray that he placed in another freezer at the other end of the room. He did all of this with a smile and when he was through, he held his hand out to Lucy as if he were turning the whole show over to her.

"Lucy'll mess up," she said. "Then she'll cry. Then everything will work out in the end." Ruby could see the whole program from start to finish. It almost set her teeth on edge.

Ruby looked down at Cyrus. The fly of his pajamas was gaping and Ruby reached down to close it so he wouldn't be exposed.

In the grey light of the TV, Cyrus' face looked like it was covered with old paste. He had a sore on his neck, right near his Adam's apple, that seemed to have been there for weeks. He said he'd gotten it shaving, but the sore didn't like like a razor cut. It was the size of a pea, round and maroon colored. It looked as if someone had pressed the burning end of a cigarette against his skin. She told him she didn't like the looks of it, but he said he'd be goddamned if he was going to pay a doctor sixty bucks to tell him he had a pimple.

Ruby was on the lookout for signs like that—lingering aches and pains, sores that didn't heal. It was the mother in her. Ruby and Cyrus had two sons. The youngest was dead—killed in a car accident ten years ago before the age of seventeen. The other joined the navy, then disappeared. They hadn't heard from him in eight years. When he was at sea, Ruby wrote him every month for three and a half years, though he never wrote back. Then one day she got a letter from the United States Naval Department that said her son had been discharged sixteen months ago and left no forwarding address and did she know his whereabouts because there were some outstanding fines and such that needed to be cleared up.

Cyrus said if he'd raised a son who went off on his own and wasn't coming back, so much the better. So he'd die and his only living son wouldn't be there to lay his father's goddamned body to rest. So he had two dead sons. Subject closed.

But Ruby thought he might come back. He might show up any minute out of the clear blue. The hope of his return set her to making pies and casseroles on holidays. It got her out of bed and dressed in the mornings.

"Maybe—" she said, almost in a whisper, "I should bake something." She turned, not to the kitchen but the front door—as if she'd heard a sound, a step on the front porch. But no. It was nothing at all, or the neighbor's cat.

Ruby went to the kitchen to make a cup of herbal tea. She started making herbal tea when she read somewhere that some instant coffees used formaldehyde. That's what she used to drink—instant coffee, six or seven cups a day. But she stopped when she found out about the formaldehyde. She started reading labels and found out that some shampoos used formaldehyde too. It was like a conspiracy—like someone was slipping small amounts of preserving fluid into people's everyday living. Now Ruby used herbal shampoo too.

Ruby put a pot of water on the stove and turned on the burner. She listened to Cyrus snoring in the other room.

"I've been trying to contact our son," she said out loud. Even if Cyrus didn't wake up and listen, she felt like hearing the sound of her own voice. "I use imagery." She closed her eyes. "I try to picture where he is—reading a newspaper, standing at a bus stop." She held her hands out like a medium. "I call to him . . . Sonny! S-o-n-n-e-e!"

She opened her eyes and listened. She could hear the TV going. Lucy was yelling, and the TV was laughing. The sound of applause rose and fell like a wave.

Ruby took a cup from the drying rack in the sink.

"I had that dream again tonight," she said. "I couldn't shut it out. Every time I closed my eyes, the dream picked up where it left off."

Ruby had read an article in the newspaper. The article said the city was digging a trench for a new water main when they came across an old coffin. Officials estimated the body had been buried over a hundred years ago in the days when a family sometimes buried their own dead and didn't always bother to have a body embalmed.

According to the article some of the coffin had rotted away and when the workers lifted the coffin out, they could see the body from the outside. The head was turned, arms and legs twisted about—as if the woman had moved inside her coffin, as if she'd torn the hair from her head!

Experts said she was remarkably well-preserved. They speculated that she had been in a deep coma at the time she was interred.

Someone had made a mistake. Someone had taken a live body and planted it six feet under. The grieving threw fistfuls of dirt on the lid and wept. They went back to their homes, sat in their rooms, and remembered the deceased over potluck and coffee. But sometime, as they walked around on top of the earth, the woman woke up.

Ruby tried to picture what the woman did then. Maybe she pressed her hands against the side and lid of the box. Maybe she called someone's name.

That's what Ruby heard in her dream. There were no pictures, only voices centuries old and words she couldn't quite make out—last words spoken from the grave like a promise or a warning, spoken to her! As if she were one of them—a living dead. A zombie!

At first there were only one or two voices speaking slowly and just beyond her. But with each dream, more voices found her. Until at last tonight her head was crammed full of hundreds of voices and ten thousand words. How they talked and talked! Urgent. Unceasing! Some whispered. Some screamed. But they all had plenty to say, and they pounded their fists and pulled their hair—old men, children, women buried with still-borns cradled in their arms. Ruby heard them all—gasping for air and gnashing their teeth. Some voices she thought she recognized. An ancestor perhaps. Or a son.

Ruby went back to the den with her cup of tea and sat on the edge of the couch, her back against Cyrus' knees. Most nights when she couldn't sleep, she sweetened her tea with honey, but this night she left it bitter. The TV was still going, and she lifted the rim to her lips and blew across the top of the liquid. She felt the steam dampen her forehead as it rose from the cup.

The conveyer belt was moving fast, and Lucy had fallen behind. She had frozen bananas piling up at the end of the belt. She was dipping bananas three and four at a time. She'd grab them up in her hands, shove them into the chocolate, then dump them into a pile on the nuts. She had chocolate on her face and smeared over one side of her hairdo. The TV was laughing, and the bananas were dropping on the floor, and Lucy was laying across the conveyer belt trying to keep the bananas from falling off.

Ruby switched off the TV, shut it off in mid laugh with Lucy stranded on the verge of her stupid terrible disaster. She sat for a long time, the tea growing tepid in its cup, the house still, and her eyes filled with tears.

Cyrus had stopped snoring. His mouth was open, but no sound came out. "Cyrus," she said. She felt her neck with her fingertips, reached out, almost touching him, and watched his chest rise without a sound.

Finishing School

The first time Jennifer Ray Dupree caught her father telling a lie, Jenny Ray was eleven years old. He said he was going to play golf all afternoon and wouldn't be back until after dinner. But Jenny Ray was out playing in the garage, and she found his golf shoes. They were right out in the open, sitting next to the water hose, and they still had dried mud in the cleats from the last time he'd played golf. His golf clubs were gone. He had remembered to take those. But the shoes were left behind, as if what he had on his mind was not golf at all but something much more important.

Jenny Ray picked up the shoes the way she'd seen her father pick them up—by hooking her fingers at the heels. She carried them to the trash can, and dropped them in.

Her mother had gone upstairs more than an hour ago, shutting the bedroom door behind her which meant do not disturb, and Jenny Ray had no intention of disturbing her. She knew that sometime in the late afternoon her mother would emerge, face flushed, touching the walls as she passed through the hallways to steady herself against her own wavering walk. Her hair would be sticking straight out at the sides and she would be licking her lips very slowly and blinking her eyes. When she looked like that, Jenny Ray stayed out of her way. If her mother came into the living room, Jenny Ray went out by the pool. If her mother came out by the pool, Jenny Ray went into the kitchen. It was like being followed by a ghostly clown. Jenny Ray's mother would never say anything when she followed Jenny Ray. Occasionally, her mother would laugh and touch her own hair with her fingers. She might even open her mouth to speak, but then she would think better of it or forget what she was about to say.

Jenny Ray studied the shoes in the trash can for a moment, as if she thought they might have something to tell her. Finally, she put the lid back on. Flies buzzed about like tiny dogfighters.

Then Jenny Ray got on her bicycle and rode to her father's restaurant a mile and a half away. She rode on the sidewalk next to the intracoastal, and from there she could see boats moving up and down the waterway and pelicans sitting on the posts that rose up at the end of a pier. Occasionally a pelican would drift overhead, and glide down to the water where it would land and bob on the waves like a piece of Styrofoam.

Jenny Ray liked being out where no one knew for sure where she was. Perhaps her mother would come downstairs earlier than usual and wonder about her. Perhaps her father would come home and worry that she had been kidnapped.

Jenny Ray's father was a rich man. He owned a restaurant called Edward's Place and made money serving people lobster and steaks and oysters on the half shell and Shrimp ala John. John was his chef. They kept the recipe for Shrimp ala John in a safe because it was worth a lot of money. Once, Frank Sinatra ate at Edward's Place. Jenny Ray's father had a picture of them together, arm in arm. The picture hung over the register behind the bar.

Jenny Ray rode past her school. It was a Catholic school and some of the students boarded there through the school year. She could see girls walking past the rectory in their plaid skirts and white shirts which they had to wear even on the weekends if they boarded. And Sister Michael was walking toward the chapel. She took huge steps across the walkway, her habit flapping about her, as if she was after someone, which she usually was. Some seagulls were gathered on the front green, and there was a lone flamingo among them. Occasionally flamingos wandered up from the intracoastal and stood about on people's lawns. From a distance they looked like the plastic ones people stuck into the ground next to their bird baths, only these would suddenly open their wings and flap off, their long legs dangling behind them.

Sister Michael was nosy. Jenny Ray concluded that nuns in general were always nosing into other people's lives because they didn't have much going on in their own. Once in class Sister Michael was lecturing on protozoans or some other microscopic organism. She was standing right next to Jenny Ray's desk and she waved her arm and Jenny Ray ducked and brought her hands up to her face, because she thought she was going to get hit. After class Sister Michael called Jenny Ray into her office and talked to her for nearly five minutes. The sister asked Jenny Ray why she had flinched so, asked her if everything was all right at home. Jenny Ray knew what Sister Michael was getting at. She was trying to get Jenny Ray to admit that she'd been hit before, that someone had knocked Jenny Ray across the face and that's why she was so jumpy. But Jenny Ray wouldn't admit to anything.

She was glad to be pedaling past the school this morning. She saw some friends in the field, playing hockey. They would knot up over the ball, their sticks clacking against one another or waving about in the air, then suddenly the ball would spurt free and the girls would trail after it. Normally, she would ride over, take up a stick and play, but this morning she wanted to find her father. She was sure he was at the restaurant. And she had something to tell him. Perhaps she would warn him that he left his golf shoes at home. Or perhaps she wouldn't say anything about that at all.

Jenny Ray could see the backside of the restaurant when she was still a quarter of a mile away. Monroe was sitting by the back door peeling potatoes. Monroe was an ex-con, a skinny black man with big bones that jutted out all over. Whenever he saw Jenny Ray, he'd smile and say, "Three squares a day!" That was a joke between him and Jenny Ray. He told her once that he had three square meals a day in prison and now he was peeling potatoes for a living. One day, Monroe would go to prison for good, for killing his wife and her boyfriend with a shotgun as they got it on in Monroe's own bed.

There were seagulls perched on the dumpster and walking about the parking lot looking for scraps and when Jenny Ray rode up she plowed right through them and they scattered and rose up in the air like a bunch of leaves caught by a gust of wind.

"Hey, Monroe," Jenny Ray said. She swung her leg around and off her bike and coasted to a stop as she stood on one pedal.

Monroe didn't answer. He just looked up at her then looked back down at his potato. He was already beginning to suspect that his wife was sleeping around, and she was on his mind all the time. His long skinny fingers held on tight to the potato as the other hand scraped at the peel. He worked with particular intensity today, as if he were skinning something alive.

"Monroe," Jenny Ray said again. She stepped on Monroe's ditty bag. It was a small leather bag he carried around with him where he kept his money and other things he said he needed. He took it with him everywhere and kept it at his feet while he peeled his potatoes, and normally if Jenny Ray so much as touched it, Monroe yelled, "Git off mah ditty bag, you spoil' white girl!"

But today he didn't even notice. He just kept doing his

potatoes and dropping them in a pot of milky water, so Jenny Ray went right past him and into the kitchen.

There, big steel caldrons of water heated up on the stoves, and a man sat at one end of a long table cracking open oyster shells. The place smelled of crab and horseradish. John was yelling at a new girl who was working salads and had chopped all the lettuce with a knife instead of tearing the leaves.

"How can you be so stupid?" he was saying. "Who cuts lettuce with a knife? Does anyone here cut lettuce with a knife?" he yelled to the kitchen. The salad girl was sobbing. Her shoulders would heave and when she sucked in air, she sounded like someone was strangling her.

"You're fired," John said. He turned his back on her. "Get out."

The girl looked at Jenny Ray as if she expected Jenny Ray to do something. Her face was red and blotchy and her eyeliner ran in stunning black rivers down her face. She pulled her apron off over her head and threw it at John's feet, then she grabbed a sweater from the back door hook and ran past Monroe and into the parking lot.

The man with the oysters looked at Jenny Ray and winked. John turned and pointed at them with a long butcher knife.

"Don't look at me," the man with the oysters said.

"You," John said to Jenny Ray, "get your tiny butt out of here."

Jenny Ray was already moving towards the door. She made her way down the hall to the dining rooms. The lights were up and the place looked all wrong. All the reds were too red and the carpet was too busy. She could see water spots on the ceiling and the paneling was marked by scrapes and dents. Joseph was behind the bar, setting up for the night. A dozen limes were spread out on the bar and Joseph was cutting them into wedges with quick strokes of his knife. He filled a glass with ice and ginger ale, then speared two cherries with a toothpick, laying the cherries across the top the way he did with an Old Fashioned. Joseph had a mustache and deep green eyes. He told Jenny Ray that she was his girlfriend and someday, if she was pretty enough, he said he would marry her for her looks and her money.

"Have you seen my father?" Jenny Ray said. She sat on a bar stool and stirred her ginger ale with her cherries.

"Hasn't been in today." Joseph was resting his elbows against the bar. Whenever Jenny Ray came in, Joseph stopped whatever he was doing, and looked right at her with those deep green eyes.

He did that with every woman who came to his bar. Jenny Ray had watched him when she was at the restaurant during hours, and had seen how women ordered drink after drink just to have Joseph look at them with those eyes.

But today she didn't notice his eyes much. "Are you sure?" she said. "Maybe he's upstairs doing the books."

"Henry's upstairs doing the books." He grabbed Jenny Ray's arm. "Don't go up," he said. "Everybody's pissed. Last night's receipts were off. Today's not a good day for you to be around. Besides, Henry hates you." Henry kept the accounts for the restaurant and looked like a crook, small eyes, greasy hair.

"I hate him too."

"Then everybody's even," Joseph said. He went back to setting up glasses. "Play me a song."

Jenny Ray knew this was a ploy, but she didn't mind. At home she had to play Mozart and Bach. Even if her mother was passed out drunk, Jenny Ray couldn't get by with a blues chord progression. Her mother would rise up like an Egyptian mummy and stand at the top of the stairs and cry out to Jenny Ray, "Please, stop that! Please!" as if Jenny Ray were torturing her. At first Jenny Ray played those kinds of chords to be mean. But then it frightened her to see her mother swaying so at the top of the stairs, and Jenny Ray worried that her mother might tumble down the stairs and break her neck.

So she liked to come to the restaurant and play at the grand piano. This is what she wanted to do someday, play through the night song after song while people drank and danced about her. She would play vaguely sad songs and take requests the way Mary did each night when people came in and wanted to sing. Mary was the piano lady at the restaurant. She was fat and impressive and wore full length dresses that must have required yards and yards of material. She had a fat voice and could play fat music and she made everyone around her feel full and unashamed. She had red hair and eyes the color of black olives—almost a purple black. She acted as if she were glad to see everyone, although inside she hated most people including herself and one day she would keel over in the midst of a performance knocking down two tables and breaking a chair and she would die, right in front of everyone, with the whole restaurant watching so that those people who still had food in their mouths found it hard to swallow.

Jenny Ray started with "Mack the Knife." Then she played "The Man From Arabi." But those songs didn't do much for her and in fact she slammed the piano cover down so hard the piano rang and Joseph from behind the bar said, "Hey!"

She ran out through the kitchen and as she went by she reached in and grabbed one of the live lobsters from the tank. She held the lobster right behind the claws and the lobster waved its many legs and curled its tail up under itself. She ran out the back door and could hear John yelling after her. Monroe was nowhere to be seen. He had sneaked off to spy on his wife. She threw the lobster into the basket of her bicycle, jumped on and pedaled as hard as she could down the walkway, not looking back.

She pedaled three blocks before she slowed down enough to look at the lobster. Its legs were still waving about but not as wildly. Its greyish green shell was already dry in the sun. It was a stupid thing to do, running off with a lobster. John would banish her from the kitchen for weeks. Her father would yell at her, but all the while he would be laughing. Henry would call her a brat to her face and remind her that lobster was the most expensive item on their menu.

She stopped at an intersection and waited for the light to change, wondering what she could do with a lobster. That's when she saw the couple in the car. It was a convertible Thunderbird, waiting across the way at the same intersection, and the top was down. The woman behind the wheel was laughing and knotting a scarf under her chin to protect her hair which was done up high on her head. The man's face was turned away from Jenny Ray. His arm stretched across the back of the seat and his hand rested on the woman's shoulder. Even from a distance Jenny Ray could see that the woman's eyes were outlined with thick black lines and her nails were long and painted bright pink.

Then the light changed and the car began to move and just as it pulled out in the intersection the man turned and looked at Jenny Ray. Their eyes met, and they recognized one another at once. He was smiling, the same smile he used when he greeted people at the restaurant bar as they came through the door in the evening. He saw her for an instant, then looked away and the car pulled on through the intersection and disappeared down the street.

Jenny Ray pushed off from the curb and coasted. She was thinking of her father's tuxedos. He had six of them, some with white jackets, some with black. They hung in his closet above his shiny patent leather shoes and on a wall was a rack of cummerbunds, black, red, paisley. There was a time when he wore a tuxedo to the restaurant every night and Jenny Ray's mother dressed in long formals and had her hair done every morning. That was when ladies and men dressed for dinner and all of the rich people from Palm Beach would drive over in their White Shadows and people drank expensive whiskeys and syrupy liqueurs from tiny glasses all night long.

But now, people didn't wear tuxedos when they went out for an evening. Jenny Ray's father wore a tuxedo only to private parties when such dress was specified.

So his tuxedos hung in the closet unused and dusty at the shoulders. When no one was around Jenny Ray would sneak up to her father's closet and slip on his tuxedo jackets one by one, each weighing heavy against her shoulders, the sleeves ending well past the length of her extended fingers, the satin lining cool against her bare arms. One after another she would put them on and stand before the mirror, the lapels slick to her touch and each smelling of faint perfumes.

A lobster claw was reaching up out of the basket. It would open and close and wave as if it were calling for help. It occurred to Jenny Ray that she had better get the lobster home and put it in her pool. When night fell, she could sneak out of the house and bicycle down to the school. Perhaps she would climb the lattice work that ran up the side of the nuns' quarters and put the lobster in Sister Michael's toilet. Or she could set it free.

She turned off of the sidewalk and pedaled down through the sand, right up to the water. The water pushed an edge of sea foam onto the sand then drew back. Jenny Ray lifted the lobster out of the basket, its claws and legs still waving, and set it on the sand. At first it didn't move. Then it dragged itself forward a bit and into the water. Then the lobster was gone.

Jenny Ray could hear boats humming as she pedaled up to the sidewalk. The sky was as blue as steel and a fish breeze was blowing up off of the intracoastal as she rolled past nuns and pelicans, swerving now and then to miss an old person with a cane. She liked to see how long she could coast without using the pedals. It was like holding her breath until her ears buzzed and her fingernails lost their color.

How the Eyes Can Play Tricks
on a Person in the Dark

It had been hot for weeks. The kind of hot that smothers a person like an old and itchy wool blanket. And so, we moved the bed outside and set it in the middle of the yard and had been sleeping out for the better part of a week.

I'll admit I felt a bit strange about it at first. Sleeping out in the wide open with my husband like that instead of locking my doors and keeping inside. But a person can only take so much heat. Then a person just doesn't care much anymore what the neighbors think or whether somebody might come along in the night meaning harm. That's the way people are in the summer in the south. Go ahead and shoot me, a person says, I'm too hot to care.

So we ask questions slower and we answer slower and nobody makes much of any kind of demand on anybody else. Once in a while somebody gets in a fight with somebody else's brother and maybe a person gets his or her head bashed in. Then everybody feels sorry for a while and just a little edgy, worrying about whether Sister sitting next to you carving up the chicken might just snap and take after everybody with the knife. But then the heat takes over and nobody even cares what Sis does with that carving knife in her free time. We all just rest under shade trees and sleep out in the yard, waiting, waiting for the heat to give.

As far as I know there is no law against bringing your bed out into your own yard. Of course we were both clothed decently and we didn't try anything romantic—too hot for that kind of thing anyway. Willie doesn't function well when the heat gets up around ninety-five degrees. And being outside did seem to help. I could be on my back and look up at the stars and lie still for as long as it took to feel the slightest breeze moving like a hand over my body and that was enough most nights for me to close my eyes, let loose of the grip I had on myself and give myself up to sleep. It gave me a feeling for the settlers and pioneers. I found sleeping outside that there's something about having

27

nothing between me and the stars, and hearing the winds moving through the trees nearby that makes me think I can keep myself alive and I'll be okay.

Willie said he had been sleeping summers outside since he was a kid. In the country, people do it all the time. He said he and his brother Randall used to ride horseback in the middle of the night when their folks were asleep. They'd ride through people's pastures and see folks in their beds right out in the open sound asleep beneath a moon too bright for sleeping sound. But sleeping out in the country and sleeping out in the city were two different things which is where we were almost—in the city that is, or a mile outside of the square and just off the highway and down a dirt road. We'd been renting there since we got married a year earlier.

So I was uneasy from the start about this business of sleeping out in the open, and thought something strange might happen because of it. But Willie said I was being stupid, that nothing would happen and if I would just loosen up some, life would be a lot more fun for both of us. At the time he said this, he looked at me like he wondered how he ever came to marry someone so edgy. And then he put some salt on his hand between his thumb and first finger, licked it, and took a shot of tequila. He drinks tequila every night. His brother showed him how when he came back on leave last Christmas from boot camp. His brother's head had been shaved since he'd joined the Marines and I couldn't help but stare at the strange knobs and ripples on his head and the kind of bluish sheen his scalp gave off. I wanted to touch his head and once he and Willie were drunk I asked if I could.

"Can I touch your head?" I said. I was sitting in a rocker watching them drink and watching the TV too. There was a murder mystery on—this advertising executive had been bludgeoned with an advertising trophy he'd won.

Willie and Randall looked at each other like I was a real stooge. Like all women were stooges and a person just had to put up with them.

Willie said, "Go on and touch his ugly head." Then he laughed and Randall laughed and I went over and put my hands on his head. I was laughing too, I'll admit. It was pretty silly, but I wanted to see what it felt like. And it felt like this: like thin wires were poking out of his blue scalp and if I looked close I could see dark little holes where the hair came out. And all those knobs and ripples were part of his skull. I had never been able to feel a skull so plainly before. Well I didn't get any big sensation

28

from it, other than the strangeness of his head and probably everybody's head. I didn't find myself wanting to touch it anymore after that.

Nothing strange happened the first three nights. Well, the first night a big red colored dog that I had never seen before came snooping around the bed, came right up and stuck his nose in my ear and sniffed and that nearly scared the living crap out of me, it being my first night and me being jumpy because of it. I'd barely begun to doze off when this big dog came up and sniffed around. I think he even raised a leg and peed on a corner of the bed, but I can't be sure because I was still half asleep. I changed the sheets next day, though.

The next two nights the only things that came around were cicadas. They are thick in the summertime when it's hot and they drone on and on day and night. They shed their skin at night and leave behind a brown shell thin as paper, sort of like rice paper toys I saw once for sale at this Chinese shop in Kansas City. The shells are perfect little bugs, but they are empty, and their backs are split open where the bugs have crawled out. In the morning you find these shells everywhere, clinging to trees and on the sides of the house. I found a few of them hanging onto our bed posts the morning after the second night. None on the sheets, but one was on the headboard just above my head.

I'm not squeamish. When I was a kid, my sisters and I used to hang cicada shells by the claws from our ear lobes and pretend we were cannibal head shrinkers, and we would tear the glowing bodies from lightning bugs and wear them on our fingers as rings until the next door neighbor, a woman who lived by herself and planted herb gardens every summer, said that might cause the lightning bugs untold pain and we might come back in our next life as lightning bugs and have the same thing happen to us if we didn't stop it. As I said, I'm not squeamish, and a big red dog is one thing, but bugs crawling out of their skins just over my uncovered head is another. So I admit I started sleeping with a hair net. I had one left over from when I was a temporary worker at the cup factory. That's where I met Willie in the first place. We dated for a month but then I got laid off. He kept asking me out anyway. After two months was up he asked me to marry him, and I decided to give it a try. If Willie had known he might be waking up to a woman wearing a hair net to sleep in, he probably would have backed out. So I waited until Willie was asleep before I put it on because he would call me an old lady and ask me if I wanted to start wearing a girdle and support hose too. If I drank some tequila with him I could pass out solid at night like he does, and I wouldn't worry about these things. But I've never been a big drinker. It's not that I'm goody-goody. It just makes me sick.

On the fourth night, I was lying in bed looking at the stars and trying to forget the heat. And about that time I remembered walking sticks. I hadn't seen one all summer, but last summer, I saw one that was so big and ugly and elegant all at once it almost made me sick to look at it. I'm talking about the living kind of walking stick. They're brown-colored and they've got spindly brown legs so they can walk about on tree bark and under leaves that litter the dirt and they look just like sticks or twigs that have fallen to the ground. The one from last summer was twelve inches long and had three sections to its body, each one marked by a knobby bumplike knot in a twig. He was clinging to the screen on the back porch door and then he fell off and I looked outside to see if he was still around and I found him next to the edge of the house. He was moving slowly, his long legs reaching out and dragging his big ugly body along. As slow as he was moving, it seemed pretty clear he was dying. It was as if he had gotten too big and ugly to stay alive. I spent the whole afternoon watching him. He got as far as the gravel drive, about fifty yards from the house and stopped.

I watched him then from a lawn chair for nearly an hour and still he didn't move. Then I went inside for ten minutes to make something cold to drink and when I got back he was gone. Nowhere to be found. Something carried him off or he dragged himself under some dead leaves out of the sun where he couldn't be seen. One of nature's mysteries. It gave me the creeps though. Knowing he was out there somewhere but couldn't be seen.

I haven't found a walking stick since and when I told Willie about him and showed him how big he was, Willie laughed at me.

"It wasn't a foot long," he said. He had his back to me as he was talking. Willie does that, talks to me with his back turned.

"It *was*, Willie. I'm telling you I saw it. Watched it all afternoon creeping around the yard."

"I haven't ever seen one a foot long," said Willie.

Well, I must admit I thought about hitting him. Not with any kind of blunt instrument. Just knocking him on the back of the head with a rolled newspaper. One time I was driving the VW van and white smoke started coming in through the air vents. Nearly choked me. I could have died from car poisoning. It was below twenty degrees and I had to drive with my window down to keep from passing out. So I went home and told Willie about it and he said, "It's never done that to me." He took it out and drove around the square a few times and then he came back and said, "I didn't see any smoke." And that was the end of it. Like the smoke never happened. I wish I could say that next the van blew up but that didn't happen. It still smokes and Willie has still never been around to see it.

So on the fourth night, I was thinking about that big ugly walking stick and how Willie didn't believe it even existed. And I was thinking that Son of Walking Stick could have been creeping around near the legs of my bed, when I saw a shadowy movement out by the road. Now as a child, I used to lie in my bed after the lights were out and stare as hard as I could at the dolls on my shelves and if I stared hard enough and long enough the dolls would start to move, ever so slightly. An arm would raise up. A head would turn just the tiniest little bit. Or their eyes would shift and they would stare back at me—as if they too suspected I was alive and were waiting for me to give myself away. But I never budged. I would lay frozen beneath my covers staring and staring at them until I'd close my eyes from pain and not open them again until morning. So I knew how the eyes could play tricks on a person in the dark. And I didn't do anything at first when I saw that shadowy movement. It could have been that crazy red dog from who knows where. But then I saw the shadow again and it was too tall to be a dog. It was a man standing behind the Rose of Sharon out by the road. I could see his white shirt in between the leaves. So I watched from where I was curled up under the sheet doing my best to look like I was asleep and he watched Willie and me from behind his bush and ever so slowly I let my hand creep up to under my pillow so I could get ahold of the claw hammer I had been keeping there ever since the first night.

That's when I heard the sound of someone humming. The song was real familiar, Battle Hymn of the Republic or maybe John Brown's Body, something like that. And I remember it gave me the same kind of feeling as looking at the walking stick—a sick but anxious feeling, like I couldn't wait to see what would happen next.

But before I could even run through all of my options this man had already come out from behind the bush, crossed the yard and climbed into bed on top of me.

His face was buried about my neck and he was humming John Brown's Body in my ear so I reached up to grab his hair with my free hand to give it a good pull so I could get enough of a breath to let out a scream. But when I reached for his hair all I

31

got was a handful of stubby bristles.

Now I've only been in a situation such as this twice before in my life—not exactly like this but situations where I had to make a quick choice. The first was when I was learning to swim at the age of seven. Actually, I was drowning. My father had thrown me in the river from the flatboat where he was fishing because I said I wanted to learn how to swim. I had surfaced for the fourth or fifth time and was throwing up river water when I saw my father's foot on the edge of the boat. He was standing in the boat, yelling for me to use my arms. So I reached up and grabbed for whatever I could get ahold of and that was my father's foot. I pulled with enough strength to turn over three boats but in this case turned over only one and my father with it and all of his tackle plus his wallet and two fishing rods. The boat and I made it to shore. Father was picked up a quarter mile downstream and the wallet, tackle and rods were never seen again.

The second time was two weeks ago when I got a sweepstakes phone call. My name had been selected by a computer from thousands to be the winner of a brand new window air conditioner and all I had to do was pick the right number out of a choice of any between one and a hundred. The lady said I had thirty seconds to respond and so after a little thought I chose the number thirty-two. And she said, "No, I'm sorry. You are incorrect. The correct number was sixty-three."

"I was going to say that," I told her. And I really was because that was the year John Kennedy died and I've always thought sixty-three was an important number, one that held a lot of cosmic weight if you believe in that kind of thing. Just goes to show you what problems changing your mind at the last minute can cause.

"But," she went on to say, "because you are a finalist you are entitled to twenty-five percent off the purchase price of one of three window units on display in our showroom."

With the smell of tequila strong about me and this man laying heavy on top of me, I could not help but think that if I had chosen the number sixty-three two weeks ago none of this would be happening. That made this choice seem all the more important and so without further thought, I pulled the hammer from under my pillow and cracked brother Randall on the head two or three times until he was out. And just to keep them guessing I pried open one of Willie's clenched fists—his fists clench when he sleeps, don't ask me why—and put the hammer in his hand. Then I packed an overnight case and walked downtown and caught the three a.m. bus heading north to Kansas City where it's cooler.

I've been staying with my sister two weeks now and Willie calls once a day asking me to come home. He's apologized six or seven times for the big fight he and Randall got in with the hammer though he swears he doesn't remember a thing. He says his AWOL brother is back in the custody of the military and that it's safe for me to return, and I'm thinking maybe I will. I've gotten a sudden sickness for anything having to do with onions or mushrooms, two food stuffs I normally like okay if not quite a lot, but if I even so much as see a picture of something with onions or mushrooms it give me sweats, and my sister seems to be stirring the two of them together for some meal or another every time I walk through the door.

It is cooler here in K.C. by a small margin, but I feel like there's something going on, some question mark growing inside of me and I have to start looking for an answer. And besides, I never thought I'd say it, but I miss the heat and living life on the edge of never knowing what's going to creep up next.

The

Things

I've

Got

Growing

Deep

Down

Inside

Sleeping Through the Night

In the middle of the night, I hear the baby cry. His cries are sharp and angry. I feel sorry for him, sleeping all alone. I know I don't like to sleep alone in the dark. Oh, we have a night light for him. It is in the shape of a kneeling angel. The angel is praying and the words at the base of the night light read, Now I Lay Me Down To Sleep. When the angel is turned on it gives off a yellow glow.

He sleeps with his head smashed up against a corner of the crib. I think that looks uncomfortable. But then, that's how he was inside of me for the last four weeks. He was turned right side up, which is upside down as far as unborn babies go. His head pushed against my ribs night and day. I could tell he was feeling cramped.

His cries are louder now, and I know he'd not going back to sleep without some help, so I get up. It's my turn. Last night, David was up with him for almost three hours. I have explained to David that when babies are teething they sometimes don't rest well. That is what it says in the books I've read, and so my mother tells me. But such facts don't make it any easier to get out of nice warm bed. It's winter time and the air feels cold so I reach for my robe.

I've known folks who bring their babies to bed with them. In fact I know a woman whose baby slept between her and her husband for three years solid. I wanted to ask her how she and her husband had sex. I mean everybody wonders such things, right? We just don't admit it. David and I say no babies in bed. It's in the best interest of our marriage, or so I've read somewhere, and David agrees. But when I see the baby all scrunched up in his corner crying and crying with his eyes shut tight, I think poor little guy. All alone in the dark.

By the time I get to his room, he's real mad. His face is red and his hair is wet from sweating. Shh, shh, I say, Momma's here. I pick him up, which I'm not supposed to do. That's why he'd not sleeping through the night. My doctor explained it this

37

way—he said to me, If you were a baby and you knew you could cry in the middle of the night and get Momma to come in and hold you and put you on her breast which is the best thing in the world as far as babies are concerned, well, what would you do? And I had to admit I would wake up and cry. The doctor said, don't go in and pick him up right away. Wait a while and if he still cries, pat him on the back. Maybe offer him some water in a baby bottle.

Once I pick him up, he stops crying. Except for little gasps now and then. His eyes are closed but he opens his mouth and kisses me—that's the way he kisses me, he just opens up his mouth and presses his lips against my face. David says that's not really kissing, but I know it is. Right now, with his eyes closed, and his little hands holding tight to my robe, I know he's kissing me.

He is still shaking a little from crying. Shh, I say, there, there. I kiss the top of his head and smell his hair. He rests his head against my breast bone and I wonder if he can hear my heart beating and if that makes him feel better.

David and I agreed that we have to try harder to help the baby learn how to fall back asleep on his own. A lady at work told David about her granddaughter who hadn't slept through the night in five years. It was because the parents picked her up every time she cried and carried her out of the bedroom to a rocker in another room. That's the way it had always been and that's the way this lady's granddaughter wanted it to stay. Well, David and I thought about going for five years without a full night's sleep. We agreed to maybe let the baby cry at night for a while.

We tried asking around to see what other people did with their babies. David asked people at work and they said, Oh, we did this or We did that or Our babies slept through the night after the first two weeks. Nobody would admit that some nights they'd just finally have to leave the baby in the room and shut the door and then hold each other down to keep from going back in and picking the baby up.

But some nights, like tonight, I can't let him cry. And the baby is grateful—he keeps kissing me and kissing me and his little hands tug at my robe. I can smell his sweet breath and it dawns on me for the very first time how someone sometime could have looked at a bunch of tiny white flowers and said those flowers are as sweet as baby's breath.

I step into the hallway and I can see David through the bedroom door. He has spread himself all the way across the bed, even over to my side, and is sleeping with his mouth open. He isn't snoring though. David rarely snores. I turn down the hallway and head for the family room. The baby starts to cry again. He is pressing his face against my shoulder which means he is looking for something to eat. Shh, shh, I tell him. You'll wake up your daddy. I squeeze the baby and pat him on the back, but by the time I've reached the rocking chair in the family room he's loud enough for the neighbors to hear and the dog comes trotting in from where he sleeps under the dining room table. The dog picks up a squeak toy that is lying by the couch. It's an orange hippopotamus with green nostrils. The dog squeaks the hippo a few times and looks up at me. But I tell him, Not now, Dizzy.

I sit in the chair and start to rock. The dog squeaks the hippo a few more times. Then he drops it and trots out of the room, disappearing down the hallway.

Sh! I tell the baby. Momma's right here. I want him to stop crying because I don't want David to wake up. David would be mad because I've broken the rules. We agreed that we would let the baby cry for five minutes before we went in the room. That's what one book suggested. If the baby was still crying then we would go in and check to make sure he's not wet or uncovered and if everything was okay then we'd pat him on the back for a while. The book said pat him on the back, then leave the room. If he still cries, go back and pat him some more, but leave the room again. That way the baby will learn to put himself to sleep.

I get up and go to the refrigerator and take out a bottle of water and offer it to the baby just like the doctor suggested. At first the baby is glad to have something in his mouth and he starts sucking right away and I think at last my problem is solved. I walk back into the family room and sit in the rocker. But then the baby opens his eyes. At first they look like shark's eyes staring at nothing or looking inside at something I can't see. Then he looks straight at me. Straight at me with a look that says, You're not going to get away with this. And he opens his mouth wide and turns his face away and lets out this big cry like I'd just stuck him with a pin. And right at the same moment the dog comes back around the corner, but this time he's got a tennis ball in his mouth and his tail is wagging. I say, Go away, Dizzy. Go away. I feel sorry for that dog sometimes.

Then I uncover my breast and press the baby's mouth against my nipple. He brings his hands up and holds my breast on either side the way he holds his juice bottle sometimes. His eyes close. One hand reaches up to touch my face. His brow is smooth and untroubled.

I listen. The house is quiet. The dog has again left the room and I suppose he is off somewhere pouting. I look out the window and notice for the first time that it is snowing. And I think, So what if we break the rules? It will be our secret.

The Neighborhood

I

Her name is Rachel. She was a kid who lived at the end of our dead end street. What I thought I might tell you about her is how she moved away. She left for California with her father. They went in a pickup truck that had only a few boxes in the back. I imagine they had her clothes and her stuffed animals. And somewhere in those boxes was a petticoat she wore around the neighborhood like it was some kind of party dress.

She was only six years old, but for a six year old person she was okay. I have a one year old baby, and Rachel was always coming over to play with my baby when she couldn't find anything else to do. She lived at the end of the street in a three-story house with her mother and her older sister. Her sister was about fourteen, and she was always driving their van to the end of the street and back.

Rachel and her mother and her sister moved in at the end of last summer. They were only leasing the house for a year. The people who own the house tried for over a year to sell it, but they were asking too much. Granted, the house is big and historical, but it's not in great shape. The paint is peeling and the wall paper is stained. I know because I took a tour with my husband once when the realtors had an open house. In fact, the whole neighborhood took a tour. The people who live across the street were coming out the door as we were going in. We all laughed and avoided looking in one another's eyes because we knew what was going on even though the realtor didn't. It was funny and sad both. I think the only people who showed up that day were people from the neighborhood who had no intention of buying but just wanted to see how their neighbors lived—what books they had on their shelves and what color towels they kept in their bathrooms.

The story was that Rachel, Mother, and Sis were going to lease with the option to buy. They moved in first and were going to work on the house until Father showed up. Father was a lawyer who lived in California.

Everyone in the neighborhood was happy to hear that someone was going to fix up the house. We hoped they were nice people who weren't noisy. But David, my husband, says he could tell right off that these people weren't stable. David is a medical technician. He works at the state V.A. hospital.

Here's what happened. Once they moved in, people were coming up and down the street all the time—two bald men, four or five kids on bicycles with dogs running loose and chasing after them. (One of the dogs was named Josie. She was a small brown dog with alert eyes, very friendly. I heard later that Josie got hit by a car and died which figures because she was always running loose.) A lady kept driving her car to the end of the street and then a little later coming back.

As it turns out, they were all related. All these relatives lived within two blocks of one another, right around the corner in fact. The two bald men were brothers of Rachel's father who was still in California. Later, when Father finally turned up, I could see the resemblance. He was bald too although he was taller. The lady in the car was an in-law.

They were all helping fix up the house. I sit out on the porch with my baby because he likes to be outside. It quiets him. Being on the porch, I could see all kinds of goings-on. One day they'd be scraping the columns on the front stoop. Then they'd be sanding. Then they'd be painting. Another day they'd have an industrial wallpaper steamer and you could see them through the windows scraping the walls in the front room.

They were making progress when one day in the midst of it all, everything stopped. No bald men. No noisy kids on bicycles. No dogs. And I haven't seen that car come down our street again. When David came home from work that night I told him about it. We were having dinner.

I passed David the pork chops. David, I said, have you noticed how quiet our street is?

David said, It is quiet. It's damn quiet.

The baby was eating turkey sticks and cheese. He loves cheese. That was the third word he learned to say after "bye" and "fish."

I said, I haven't seen that lady in the car all day. That lady makes at least a dozen trips a day up and down this street.

Maybe they're resting, David said.

I watched the baby mash a turkey stick on the table and didn't answer. But I thought to myself, this is different. I could tell people weren't resting down there at the end of the street.

II

The neighborhood stayed like that for two days. Quiet.
Outside of David and me and the baby, everybody else on the
street is over forty. We have three widows, an unmarried school
teacher, a couple in their sixties who never had children, and
two fellows who live together in the house across the street.

Then on the third day a police car came and parked down at
the end of the street in front of the house. I was sitting on my
porch and looking back I think I must have been waiting for
something like this. The mother came out of the house. Right
away she was talking loudly. And waving her hands at the
policeman. I did catch a few words. Keep him away! I don't
want him on this street! she said. I could hear that part. Rachel
came out on the front porch then, and the mother stopped
talking. The mother yelled for Sis—that's what they called the
fourteen year old—and sent them both up the street. They walked
by my house and I could hear Rachel say, Who's Momma talking
to?

Sis said, She's just talking to some friends.

The policeman got back in his car and came driving slowly
back up the street. He even looked at me as he drove by. He
studied me. A young mother with a baby in her lap. You know
how police make you want to stand up and yell, Don't look at
me! I didn't do anything! That's what I felt like doing.

About twenty minutes later Josie came trotting down the
street, towards Rachel's house. Josie was the dog who would later
get run over by a car. At the time I didn't realize that drama was
unfolding before my very eyes. But here comes Josie and after
Josie comes a boy on a bicycle. I recognized the boy. He was one
of those who came down on his bicycle when the families were
pitching in to fix up the house. He was maybe thirteen, a bit
chubby and had blond hair that was spiked. I think those spike
haircuts make the kids look mean. I guess that's what they want.
He called after the dog. Josie! he said. Come on, girl!

Then he stopped his bicycle in front of my house and stared
down the street. He sat that way for a long time, didn't move a
muscle. By this time Josie had wandered back home. She wasn't
anywhere to be seen. But the boy wasn't looking for Josie. He
was just staring at Rachel's house.

Just at that moment I looked down. My baby was biting my

toes. He's taken to doing that lately. I can't go barefoot around my own house. He doesn't do this to his father, only to me. If I curl my toes under so he can't get them, then he bites the top of my feet. So he was biting my toes, and I yelled, Ouch! which made the baby laugh. Cut that out! I said. I shook my finger at him and looked stern. No biting, I said.

When I looked up again, I saw Rachel's mother flying by on a bicycle. It was a kid's bike so her knees practically touched her chin every time she pumped the pedals. She had on a bathrobe and under that a nylon nightgown. The bathrobe flapped behind her as she blew down the street, chasing after the blond-haired boy. I caught a glimpse of him just as his bike tore around the corner. She pedaled as hard as she could, but he was too fast for her.

When she got to the corner, she stopped her bike and stood up, straddling the bike between her legs. She opened up her mouth and yelled as loud as she could so everyone would hear, You keep your child-molesting son away from my house!

She yelled the exact same words a second time. Then she sat on the bicycle and pedaled back down the street. I looked at my baby. I can be nosy but I don't stare at people when they've cut themselves loose like that.

The baby was playing with a golf ball. He would throw it on the concrete, then crawl after it. Ball, he would say once he got it back. He'd shake the ball a few times then throw it again.

III

School started and an entire winter went by. When snow and icy winds set in, people don't work much on neighborhood relations. It's enough to get out of bed and put your feet to a cold floor. Around here winter only lasts four months which is not as bad as what people put up with farther north. I'm not a cold weather person. I wrap myself up with scarves and heavy coats and thick stockings, but I'm still cold. Cold fingers, cold feet. The longer winter gets the farther up my arms and legs cold travels until I think I'll lose my mind or freeze to death. I imagine someday I'll die in the winter.

So I'm always glad when March comes. Crocus start to bloom and not long after that come daffodils and a person can start to look around the world again and think of something else besides keeping warm. I'd only seen Rachel and Sis and Mother from a distance up until March. They'd pass by my house in their van on the way to or from school, to or from the store. My baby and I would look out at them through icy windows. And I'd see that from their van they were looking back at us.

As far as I could tell, work never did start up again on the house once it had stopped. I suppose they spent the winter with walls half painted. And Father, the lawyer from California, didn't show up either. At least I never saw him. Maybe he sent his family out here and never intended to follow them. Or maybe once they were gone, he realized how glad he was to be alone.

Anyway, it wasn't until March that I really got to know Rachel. At first I didn't like her. She was always cutting through my yard. I never did that as a kid, cut through people's yards. But Rachel was always wandering around other people's yards looking for something to do. She didn't have any riding toys or a swingset. And I never saw the mother out playing with her. Except for that one time when she blew down the street in her nightgown on Sis's bicycle, I never saw the mother out on her own two legs.

Rachel would cut through my yard and walk right past my dining room window which made my dog crazy. My dog is good, but he barks at people who cut through our yard, especially meter readers and children. Before I could do anything about it, Rachel would walk past my window, the dog would bark like someone had walked off with his tail, and the baby would wake up from his nap and cry.

My baby is not a sleeper. Every night we are like wrestlers, me trying to pin him down to sleep, him fighting to stay awake. When he gets really sleepy he starts hitting me. He knocks his head against my breast bone.

My baby taught me how to like Rachel. He didn't care if she cut through yards, or lived in a half-finished house, or wore clothes that didn't match and left her shoes and stockings wherever they might come off. Whenever he was playing on the porch and she came around the corner (it must have seemed like magic the way she appeared from nowhere) he would drop his toys and hold his arms out to her and smile. And if she got bored with him and left to chase a stray dog or pick flowers from somebody's garden, my baby would cry and cry and sometimes I couldn't get him to stop until we went inside and I gave him a cookie.

Rachel was good with my baby. Jason, she'd say. Jason, watch. And then she'd make a face or some funny noise and baby would laugh. She liked to play with baby toys and talk baby talk. But sometimes she'd carry his toys off into other yards or fill his little boxes up with mud. And one time I caught her placing his juice bottle up on a window sill where he couldn't reach it, and he was crying and hitting his own face with his hands.

I told Rachel that she mustn't do things like that because babies can't help themselves. That's cruel, I told her.

What's cruel mean? she asked.

Cruel means you do something to hurt someone on purpose.

David says it's hard to tell with a case like Rachel's. Maybe the chubby boy on the bike did something to Rachel. Maybe he didn't.

IV

My baby has been slow to walk. Lately, he gets in a squatting position and pushes himself up to where he is standing. He'll stand for a few seconds, look around. Oh! Oh! he'll say. He knows already that the world is a different place when you're on your own two feet. When I see my baby standing up with nothing to grab onto I am breathless at what he'll do next.

Rachel started peeking in our windows in late spring. Maybe it seems like a little problem. But it's hard enough to have privacy on a dead end street without kids window peeking all the time. We were eating dinner the first time. She came right up to our dining room window which is low to the ground and pressed her face against the screen. Hello! she said. I see you in there!

My dog went nuts.

David said to ignore her and we kept on eating and finally she went away. But the very next day she was back again. Hello in there! she said.

David got up from the table and went outside. He said something and Rachel left.

What did you say to her? I asked when he came back in.

I told her to stop peeking in our windows, he said.

We thought that would take care of the problem, but it didn't. Two days later she was peeking in our bedroom window. It was afternoon and I was folding laundry that I'd dumped out on the bed. I had all my clothes on which is not always the case. Sometimes I run around the house in my underwear. I half dress then get busy changing a diaper or answering the phone. Jason was on the bed playing in the clean clothes. He'd grab a shirt and wave it like a flag over his head then throw it on the floor.

He had pushed a whole pile of sorted underwear on the

floor, and I was bending down to pick it all up, when I had a feeling. Someone was watching me. It's the same way you feel when you've been caught in a lie. It hits people in different places—stomach, neck muscles. I feel it in the back of my legs.

Once, before the baby was born, I had this same feeling. I was taking a bath in the middle of the day with the bathroom door open, and from the corner of my eye I saw a man's face in the bedroom window across the hall. I sat up straight, looked at the window, but no one was there. The window sheers breathed in and out. I climbed out of the tub, dripping and naked, and locked all the doors in the house.

This time when I looked up I caught Rachel's face framed in the window. She had her hands cupped at either side of her face and her nose was pressed against the screen. I walked over to the window, bent down so my face was even with hers, and she didn't even look embarrassed or run away.

Wait right there, Rachel, I said. I want to talk to you.

My mind was going now. I didn't care if the father did dump them, or if that boy did do something to Rachel. There are lines that people do not cross, and we are supposed to learn about these lines early on. I put my baby on my hip. I was going to tell Rachel why peeking in other people's windows is wrong.

But when I got outside, Rachel was gone. At first I thought she had gotten scared and run home, but when I walked around the corner of the house I saw she'd just moved to another window to get a better view.

I had walked up behind her, taken in enough air for a long speech and opened my mouth, when Rachel turned around and took my baby's outstretched hand.

Did you hear the tornado last night? she said.

I ignored the question. Rachel, I said, You mustn't peek in our windows.

Rachel was clapping hands with the baby, but her face was solemn. I heard it, she said. I was scared.

It's true we get our share of tornadoes in the springtime here. I can remember as a kid waking up to a room blue with electricity and the air smelling like wet metal. A few years ago a teenager was killed in a tornado. She pulled her car over to the side of the road and crawled in a ditch, but the storm picked her car up and threw it down on top of her. The tornado bounced through a whole street of houses and crumpled them up like paper. We only had a tree come down. David and I were thrown out of bed by the crash. It missed our bedroom window by inches, and the next morning David took a picture of me

47

standing between the stiff arms of the tree. In the picture I look like the tree's arms have got a hold of me and won't let go.

But there wasn't any tornado the night before. Rachel must've had a bad dream. It might've rained and there might've been some lightning and thunder. I've slept through storms like that. But I've never slept through any tornado.

I put Jason on the ground at my feet and got down on my knees to where I was face to face with Rachel. I took her by the arms and said, Listen, if I catch you peeking in our windows again, I'll—I thought for a minute about what I could say that would show her I meant business. I'll call the police, I said. I held her arms a little more tightly. Peeking in people's windows is against the law, Rachel.

She looked straight at me, and I could tell she knew what I was saying. But some kids just won't admit that they've been caught.

My father says there aren't any tornados in California, she said. Earthquakes, but no tornados.

Rachel had this stubborn look on her face—the kind of look kids get when someone's about to hit them, and they don't care. The kind of look that says nothing you can do will hurt me.

Right then, something went off in my head. I can't claim any good reason for why it was so important to make my point, except that there I was down on my knees trying to tell her something, like there was something big at stake here. My neck was starting to feel hot and itchy.

So I did something mean. I don't know why, but I told Rachel that a long time ago, a man was murdered in her house. I wanted to make her feel afraid. I wasn't lying. There really was a man murdered in her house. The man's name was Stinger and at the turn of the century he was an important banker. It wasn't a messy unsolved murder where arms and legs were cut off and buried about the neighborhood. Some guy was unhappy because Stinger wouldn't give him a loan, so the man came to Stinger's home and shot him.

I told Rachel that Stinger died in the attic. But he probably died in the front hallway or some place like that.

Rachel was quiet for a long time. She was quiet for so long that I got embarrassed and couldn't look her in the eye. I let go of her arms.

At last she pointed at something behind me and said, Jason's eating dirt.

V

A few days went by. The next time I saw Rachel she was wearing a lacy petticoat and a lavender sweater. She came up to the porch where my baby and I were playing and said, What does this look like? She held the petticoat skirts out and twirled around.

I said, It looks like a petticoat to me. But Rachel had never heard of the word petticoat.

It's a slip, she told me.

Oh, I said.

I thought petticoat was a much prettier name. But I didn't tell her that. Instead I said, Aren't you hot in that sweater?

Rachel ignored me and sat down on the steps to play with the baby. I'm going to California to live with my dad, she said. We're going to plant watermelons. We're leaving tonight so I need to play outside as much as I can because I'll be in the car a long time.

This was the first I'd heard of any trip to California, so I didn't know whether to believe her or not.

How come you're going to California? I said.

Rachel handed Jason a small plastic block and watched him shake it and throw it on the ground. I just am, she said.

I watched as Jason reached out and grabbed a handful of Rachel's hair. When he pulled her hair, she made a face and the baby laughed. Stop, she said. She pried his fingers loose from her hair, and he laughed and reached for her again. I felt sad for the baby. If Rachel did go to California, he would miss her.

Then out of nowhere Rachel said, How big is Jason's room?

I don't know, I said.

I mean, is it big or medium or small, Rachel said.

It's medium, I answered.

My mother gave Sis the biggest room in the house. Then I have the next biggest and Momma has the smallest room of all, she said.

In this house, all the bedrooms are upstairs. The big bedroom goes all the way across the front of the house. I think it used to be two bedrooms, but a previous owner knocked out a wall. The other two bedrooms are at the back of the house. Both are small. But the smallest one is more like a closet or a cell than a bedroom. A person could barely fit a twin bed in there. I remember saying so when I took the open house tour.

That was nice of your mother to give you the bigger room and keep the smallest room for herself, I said.

49

Momma loves that little room, Rachel said. She says it's like a tree house up there. She pretends she's up in the trees when she looks out the window. Sometimes we can't even get her out of bed. She stays in that little room all day long.

I pictured Rachel's mother lying in bed in that tiny room, looking out the window at the trees, not wanting to get up. And all at once I felt bad for Rachel. I felt bad for all of them—Rachel, the mother, Sis, even their big black dog.

After that, Rachel went home. A little later in the afternoon I saw Rachel and her mother outside. Rachel was still in her petticoat and her mother was taking pictures. Rachel would stand before a tree and hold the skirts of her petticoat out and smile. Then the mother would snap the picture. Rachel would strike another pose and the mother would take another picture. And then the mother just kept snapping pictures even when Rachel stopped posing, even when Rachel stepped out of the frame.

Just before dinner Rachel came down and got our phone number. She was going to call Jason once she got to California. I tried to explain to her that the baby didn't know yet to talk into the phone. Whenever I put the receiver to his ear he just listens and breathes. But Rachel insisted he would talk to her. I bet he'll laugh, if I tell him some jokes, she said.

When night came, I went outside to walk my baby to sleep. I've taken to doing that lately since the weather's been nice. I wrap him in a flannel blanket and go outside just as it's getting dark. The tree bats are coming out, and we watch as they flutter through the sky. I walk up and down the street, and my baby and I hold onto one another against the dark. Sometimes it takes an hour before his eyes finally close and his head rests on my shoulder.

When we started to walk on this night, I noticed right off the pickup parked in front of Rachel's house. It had those few measly boxes in the back. My baby seemed especially willing to go to sleep, and I'd barely got to the end of the street and back before his head was on my shoulders and his eyes were nearly closed. He was humming to himself the way babies do.

That's when all of a sudden Rachel's porch light came on and they all spilled out of the house. A man—I suppose he was Rachel's father—Sis, the mother, and Rachel. All of them tumbled out of the house at once. The passenger door was opened and Rachel climbed in. The man came around and got in behind the wheel.

Bye, sissy, bye! I heard Sis yelling from the porch step. I love you, sissy! she said. Her voice was high and wavered from tears.

The mother stood by Rachel's side of the car for a moment, then stepped back. The truck started and the lights flicked on. The mother and Sis turned back to the house and the pickup made its way up the street.

I stepped off the road, walked up my driveway. I felt bad being there, felt like I'd witnessed some terribly private thing. But even so, as the pickup passed I turned to look. I hoped maybe Rachel might wave. But I couldn't even see her through the window. She was slumped way down, or maybe she was resting her head in her daddy's lap.

I went inside and put my baby down in his crib. The air was warm and still and already he had sweat on his little nose.

Later, when I was lying in bed, I thought about my baby, and Rachel, and how once an old man put his hands on me. He was a farmer who owned some horses which he sometimes let my friend and me ride. I never told anyone, and once he put his hands on me, I never went back to ride his horses again. I don't think about that old man very often. And when I do, it's as if he put his hands on some other little girl and not on me at all.

After I'd gotten in bed, David crawled under the covers. I love the feel of his smooth skin when he first gets into bed and pulls me up next to him. He was feeling romantic on that particular night, and he started to kiss me. The window was open and a breeze was blowing in which made the open blind click against the window sill. David kept kissing me and I kept thinking about those open blinds, not that I thought someone was looking in, but sometimes I get an idea in my mind and I can't get it out or concentrate on anything else.

So finally I said, David would you shut the blinds? And he didn't get mad or laugh at me. He's real good to me that way.

Without a word he reached over and dropped the blinds—so that no one could see us.

Whatever a Sleepless Night Brings

It was the eighth night in a row that David and I had made love, and all I could think about was pileated woodpeckers. Now I know what the word pecker means and before anyone starts making any psychological diagnosis, let me make it clear that I think both I and woodpeckers are above such notions.

I didn't know what pileated meant though so I looked it up once. The dictionary didn't tell me much but it did say that pileated came from a Latin word pileus, which means felt cap. When I read that, I started thinking about the Romans and wondering if they wore felt caps. I've never seen any pictures of them in felt caps, just sandals and togas. But there must have been some Roman some time who wore a felt cap or at least knew somebody else who wore a felt cap, otherwise why would they bother to come up with a word like pileus? Then I wondered who it was that gave the pileated woodpecker its name and I decided it was a good name, even though most people don't have any idea what the word pileated means and never bother to find out.

I was making love to my husband and thinking about pileated woodpeckers and felt caps and Romans and scientists. I had seen two pileated woodpeckers just a week before in the forest. David and my three year old son Jason and I were hiking through the woods to a waterfall and two of them flew side by side right in front of me. They both hooked on to the trunk of a tree about twenty yards away and one of them pecked at the trunk a bit before we startled the other and they both flew off, deeper into the woods where they couldn't be seen. They were big and quiet and they held their wings out and more glided than flew.

We have some small woodpeckers in our neighborhood. The trees are big and old here so they're full of ants and bugs and woodpeckers like bugs of course. I wake up to the sound of them every spring morning. The birds around here sometimes start singing as early as three o'clock in the morning—sparrows and cardinals and wrens and mourning doves. My husband nearly hates it—they get so loud they wake him up and go on for hours and he can't get back to sleep. But I love to be under a thin sheet, naked with the sky half lighted out my window and the birds going crazy. Sometimes it gets so loud that I almost want to yell and stand up and shake my head out, but I like that feeling too. I like to listen to the birds. There aren't any words to what they way. And I get tired of words because they are constantly running through my head, a stream of them, a voice inside me talking and remembering everything there is to remember. Even at night when I sleep, this voice keeps talking and when the birds make their noises, I am grateful because I can listen to their sounds, shut the words off for a while. This far south though it gets too hot to leave the windows open all summer long. David can't sleep in the heat. He tosses and turns and sweats until the sheets are soaked like he's got a fever, but the fever is outside not inside. So around the end of June we shut up the windows and close all the doors and turn on the air conditioner. I can barely even hear the birds then. David sleeps peacefully in the cool house air and I toss and turn all night listening for sounds I cannot hear.

But on this night, the windows were still open though it was too early in the night for bird sounds, and all I could hear were cars driving up and down the street and two blocks away, a train sliding through the night, and in the next room, Jason grinding his teeth.

We were trying to get pregnant. That's the way it is said these days. We were trying to get pregnant. We wanted to have a baby. But as far as I can tell, I was the only one who would get the stretch marks and the swollen feet.

We were being very premeditated about the whole thing. I had been marking my calendars and we had figured out the most likely times. And now for eight nights in a row, David loaded up my universe with millions of sperm, and we thought that surely one of the fragile little things would worm its way through. Then an egg somewhere inside of me would take the lonely fellow in.

That was how we did it with Jason. Everything very deliberate and all. But somehow that was easier—the blind leading the blind, if you know what I mean.

I am lying on my side now and David is asleep. I press my palm against his bare back. He doesn't move. I am wondering why I feel so bad. The night has passed into a deep darkness that admits no sounds. Even the crickets have gone silent. I have the whole world to myself.

Usually, I don't mind it so much when I can't sleep. I get up and if it's cold, I put on a robe or if it's not I pull a sheet out of the linen closet and drape it over my bare skin and I haunt the rooms of my own house. This is when the rooms are all mine. I don't have to share them with anyone.

But tonight I don't feel like getting up. A voice is running on and on. It passes over everything I have seen and done for the day, for other days: Today was windy and the trees shook themselves out in the wind, bending and bending then breaking free . . . I pressed some stones into the dirt at the edge of my garden . . . my father is dead now for years . . . I lock myself into my house at nightfall . . . I have two sisters older than I . . . we speak on the phone and sometimes find we have little to say . . . I plant heather and snap dragons and hope when the summer grows too hot for me to care anymore, these flowers can save themselves . . .

Then I know by the wetness on my face that I must be crying. I don't know why. I can't hear my own breathing or even the sounds of others sleeping nearby and I reach out and put my warm hands on David's bare skin and in spite of the fact that he doesn't move, I pull myself close to him, press my face against his back, and feel like I'm being taken over and I want to shake him for his peaceful sleeping. I'm hoping something will happen. I'm hoping something will save me.

At first there is nothing. I wait for the sound of something other than the voice in my head. I wait for hours like this, holding on to the nearest warmth.

Then at last I hear one bird singing, and something is started.

Waiting

for a

Word

or a

Sign

Sweetness and Heat

Esther was sitting in a field next to the spot where a ship from outer space had landed last fall, at least that's what Tess and Esther decided since nothing else could explain the sudden appearance one morning of a large circle of burned grass that didn't fade for a full three months. Esther and Tess had held vigils there every night for the first week, then once a week or so until it got too cold to continue and now since it was nearly a year later and the circle was no longer visible, there didn't seem to be any point. Beside her was a shoe box with a live tree bat inside. She was waiting for Tess and Dirty Rogers to show up because they had all planned to sneak down to the junk yard and search for ball bearings.

Tess and Dirty were twins out of a family of eight brothers and sisters. They both had red hair and freckles. Tess was tall and thin and her red hair was long and wavy and about as beautiful as any red hair Esther had ever seen. She hadn't ever cut her hair—ever, even though all her older sisters had short hair and every three months or so the Rogers took all eight kids into town to get haircuts—the boys got crewcuts and the girls got bobs to cut down on the likelihood of head lice. But Tess threw a fit at age four the first time they took her down to get a haircut. She ran away and hid in the well house all night and didn't come home until lunch the next day. She got a beating for running off, but she said she'd do it again if they tried to cut her hair off, or she'd do something else, something more drastic—jump in the well or run away with the next revival show that came through town—and something in her clear green eyes must have told them she meant what she said because from then on they left her alone. Whenever the family loaded up the station wagon for haircut day, they left Tess sitting on the porch by herself. No one even asked her to come along.

Tess had perfect green eyes. Perfect for staring a person down—not in a hateful way, but in a patient way that made a person feel like she needed to go home and rethink her whole reason for being alive. Her eyes were almost transparent so that if Esther stared into them long enough she thought she could see Tess's thoughts hung out like clothes on a clothes line. Esther and Tess used to practice staring into each other's eyes because they thought if they did it enough they could learn to read each other's minds and then they wouldn't even have to speak to one another, like in the science fiction stories with advanced civilizations that visit earthlings and have dispensed with old-fashioned speech because they can send their messages by way of mental telepathy. They were getting pretty good at it too. At certain times, Tess could look at Esther or Esther could look at Tess and each knew exactly what the other was thinking.

But Tess complained that Esther's eyes were muddy and hard to read and Esther, when she studied herself in the mirror with her brown hair and brown eyes, had to agree. What Esther wanted out of life was long red hair and clear green eyes and milky skin that burned easily but always looked soft and cool and was covered with fine blond hair. And when Tess wasn't looking, when they were sitting near the top of a sycamore tree and Tess was staring out at the horizon watching for vultures, or when they were hiding from Dirty—behind the well house showing one another scars on various parts of their bodies and making up stories of how they got there, Esther would study Tess's skin and wish to touch it lightly with her fingertips to see if it was in fact as smooth and cool as it looked.

Dirty's real name was Chester, but only his very old grandmother who smelled of cough syrup called him that. Even his mother called him Dirty. To look at him, he wasn't any dirtier than any other kid in the family, but he had this smell about him. It was more than just a sweaty boy smell. He had the smell of something that had been wadded up and lost under a piece of furniture for years. His mother was always after him to take a bath. In fact, he was probably the cleanest kid of the whole family because she was always grabbing him up and throwing him in the tub, even though she'd just washed him the day before. She couldn't keep track of who had washed when and every time she'd get after one kid or another to take a bath, they'd nearly always tell her without blinking an eye, "It's Dirty's turn," and they'd go on with their playing.

Tess and Esther let Dirty hang around with them since he was Tess's twin brother. But he was the kind of kid most everyone else in the neighborhood made up stories about. One story Tess had heard from her ugly cousin Philip was that Dirty liked to eat mud from a spoon. But Tess assured Esther that this

58

was not true. Once, she said, when they were very young Tess had made a mud pie and had stolen some cake sprinkles from the kitchen and decorated the pie very nicely and she had persuaded Dirty to take a large bite which he spit out all over her dress front. But that was the limit of his mud eating.

Dirty was really a very generous fellow and often traded good pieces of junk with Esther. And Tess told her once that she thought Dirty had a crush on Esther, but Esther discouraged any romance although once she showed Dirty her underwear so that she might see his penis since she had never seen one before, being an only child with no brothers around. Dirty didn't seem to notice that the showing was not fair and square since Esther wouldn't go any farther than her underwear. And Esther made him swear that he wouldn't tell anyone, not even Tess, and if he did she had an aunt who was a certified witch who could make her head spin around three hundred and sixty degrees and specialized in tortures for young boys and Esther would have her make up a spell that would cause all of his sex organs to shrivel. So far, this was enough to keep him quiet, although Dirty seemed not to give it another thought anyway, and didn't ever sneer or tease Esther or act like they'd done anything especially monumental or wrong. And for this she felt obligated in friendship to him. He had shown her his private self and had not expected anything in return. She wouldn't sit next to him on the bus riding to school, or anything like that, but when the bullies started to make fun of him, she didn't laugh with the other kids. She looked the other way, out the window, or pretended to read a book, so that he wouldn't feel like she was watching him in his public shame.

She had been waiting for them for nearly a half an hour, and her head was beginning to feel big. This happened to Esther every once in a while. She would be in a church pew or in the reading group at school or just sitting and waiting for something and all of a sudden her head seemed to expand and she felt huge and prehistoric. Her head bones got chalky and porous. Each molar grew to the size of a dinner plate and if she happened to be chewing something at the time, the grinding of her teeth echoed in her cavernous head. Sometimes her body would get big too, and she would be as big as a two story house and her legs would be as long as a couple of cars and she could barely move for being so big.

At first when she felt such a condition creeping up, it was odd and interesting, but when it came upon her in a place such as a church or at school when the teacher was looking right at her, it was all she could do to keep from letting out a scream or falling on the floor and rolling about.

This big business all started when she had seen a woman once at the train depot, where her great-grandmother always departed on long winding trips across the country to visit her youngest son in California. (Great-grandmother never flew, always took the long silver passenger train pointed northwest on the track with its small round windows through which Great-grandmother would peer at Esther and wave a gloved hand each time she departed.) This woman sat beneath an enormous station clock on one of the long wooden benches by herself with bags placed all about her feet, and Esther stared and stared at her. The woman's ankles were huge swollen pithy things as big as tree stumps. Esther's mother said it was elephantiasis which came from having worms and that should teach Esther to always wash her hands and to line the toilet seat with paper in public restrooms.

Esther had giantess nightmares. She read encyclopedia articles on elephantiasis and worried about parasitic blockage in her lymph ducts and wished she had never gone to the train station ever and seen that miserable overgrown woman.

Now she could feel her head growing, and the grass was getting itchy beneath her legs, and she was ready to give up the wait and go home before she got so big that she didn't want to move, when Tess and Dirty appeared across the field, cutting through a grove of cottonwoods that held the skin and bones of at least five kites. Those cottonwoods always shipwrecked a dozen or so kites before the summer's end.

Esther could tell that Tess was mad or had an idea about something, even from across the field. It showed in the way she walked. Tess had long freckled legs and when she was mad or had some dangerous thought in her head, she took great long strides and swung her arms high, almost like she was marching. Dirty trotted along beside her, carrying a cloth laundry sack which he used whenever he went to the junk yard. He had long legs too and this was still a couple of years before he had his foot cut off by a train. After he lost his foot everyone said wasn't it a shame because he had such long legs and who knows, maybe he could have been a good runner, maybe a state champ in something if only he'd had the chance.

Esther lifted the shoe box with the bat and let it rest on her lap. She shook it gently and heard the bat thump against the sides and claw about. She found it the night before lying in the grass by a tree. She had gotten father's leather gloves and had scooped it up with her hands and kept it in the shoe box in her closet throughout the night and hadn't had a chance to show it to anyone yet. Esther didn't tell her mother she had found it, much less caught it because her mother would start gagging right off and talk about disease and tell her she would get rabies and they'd have to chain her up to the back of the house while Esther frothed at the mouth and pulled out her hair.

This is what her mother always claimed whenever Esther came into contact with anything from nature, which made Esther all the more inclined to capture any creeping thing that crossed her path. Sometimes, if it wasn't something she thought would bite, she would let it crawl up her arms and even into her hair. Walking sticks, praying mantises, garter snakes. Stink bugs, june bugs, black beetles. Even Tess who was accepted by the boys of the neighborhood and could swim faster than any of them and would jump into the river from the highest rock at Flat Creek, even Tess would shiver at the thought of touching some of the things that Esther would touch. And whenever anyone in the neighborhood found some great ugly bug they'd always run off in search of Esther, collecting other kids as they went so that by the time they found Esther and Tess there might be a whole parade of kids and Esther would calmly retrieve her leather gloves from under the front porch steps and pull them on like a surgeon and they would all march to the site where the creature was held captive, encircled by this time by a ring of kids.

It wasn't much, but it was all Esther had, and it kept her from being a creep or a nobody so she kept it up, even though it almost made her sick to touch some things, slugs in particular. Later, after the teachers divided everyone into groups of boys and girls and marched them all down to see sex education films in separate gyms, none of this mattered. When the boys and girls regrouped in their homerooms after talk of spermatozoa and menstruation and the like, it was clear that now the rules had changed. Esther could almost taste it in the air. She could see it in the way that the boys glanced about out of the corners of their eyes, first at one another, and then at this girl or that. Girls now were creatures who grew breasts and who had monthly things happen to them and their excellence was judged on something altogether different somehow. And Esther, when that day came, would feel as though she was being transformed without her permission into something foreign from what she had at first planned.

"We're going to move into a funeral home," Tess yelled when she was halfway across the field.

61

Esther had heard such declarations before. Tess's father was often starting off on some new job. One month he would be off selling trumpets in Texas and preparing to move the whole family to some warehouse above a music store and the next he would be down in Florida working a carnival and trying to find a backer to invest in a traveling concession stand. Every three months or so he would reappear and wander about the yard calling out the kids' names as if he was trying to remember which name belonged to which face. He would order everybody around and complain about how his eight children were cut loose all over the countryside, and he couldn't keep track of who was who much less where anybody was. He would make everybody put on shoes and load everybody up for their haircuts. Then, in another morning or two he would be gone again, and for a half day or so everyone in the family including Tess and Dirty would just lie about the house or yard trying to recover.

"It's true," said Dirty. "Dad's going to be a grave digger."

"A *keeper*," said Tess. "A graveyard keeper. He won't dig the graves. He'll just keep the grounds up and mow around the gravestones. That's what he said."

"And we're going to live in the funeral home with dead bodies," said Dirty. They were close enough now that they were both walking. And Esther from where she was sitting could see that Dirty's eyes were big and round. He was already terrified and they hadn't even packed their bags yet.

"He'll be there in case the funeral home gets any calls in the middle of the night," said Tess. She dropped on the grass beside Esther and began to examine a large red scab on her right knee.

"What's in the box?" said Dirty.

"A bat," Esther said and she handed him the shoe box without even looking at his face. She was studying Tess to see just how serious she was about all this graveyard business. "Be careful," Esther said, without much conviction. She could see by the way Tess's cheek muscles were flexing that Tess was clenching and unclenching her teeth. "It might have rabies."

"So," said Tess without looking up from her knee, "you and me and Dirty are walking to Whitaker-White Funeral Home. I checked the paper this morning and they've got at least two bodies there. I want to see what it's like."

"We can't go in a funeral home dressed like this," Esther said. She looked at Dirty who was shaking the shoe box. "Stop shaking the box so much," she said.

"It's dying anyway," Dirty said. "You ought to let it go so it can die in peace."

Esther looked back at Tess. "They won't let us in. And besides we don't even know those dead people." It gave Esther an uneasy feeling to think about looking over the body of a dead person she didn't even know. Like she was watching someone undress and wash themselves without that person knowing it. Being dead and lying about in a casket seemed a very private thing.

"We'll say we know one of them," Tess said. She pulled a newspaper clipping from her pocket and handed it to Esther. "I brought each of us a hanky," she said, pulling those from her pocket too. She gave Esther one with the initials D.F.R. on it and Esther wondered who had blown their nose out on this hanky before she got ahold of it. "Dirty said he'd come, said it wouldn't bother him one bit."

Esther glanced at Dirty. He had the lid off and was studying the bat as close up as he could without touching it. Esther knew that old Dirty was probably about to pee in his pants at the thought of looking over a strange dead body and if he went, he would probably wake up in the middle of the night from nightmares for the next two months.

Esther looked at the clipping in her hand. It was about a thirty-three year old woman named Eugenia Louise Stoner who had gone to meet her maker at 3:43 a.m. Tuesday after a long illness. She had been a member of this and that church and was survived by so and so relatives and that was about it.

"I thought it might be good to see a young one," Tess said. She too was looking at the clipping in Esther's hand. "You can find an old dead body anywhere. But a young one—"

"My mother says there's nothing more terrible than seeing a young person lying dead somewhere," said Dirty. He had put the lid back on the box and had the box resting on his knees as he rocked back and forth, squatting on his haunches. That's how Dirty always sat. Not all the way with his butt to the ground, but hunkered down part way, as if, in case of some emergency, like if someone came along looking for a weak body to beat on, Dirty could spring up and run away.

Esther wasn't concerned about seeing a dead body. She'd seen a few—an emphysemic uncle, and a great-grandmother who was ninety-three when she finally croaked and had looked and smelled half dead for as long as Esther could remember even before she finally let loose of life and closed her eyes once and for all.

It was more that Esther didn't like getting caught doing things she knew her mother would make a big fuss over. And

63

lying their way into a funeral home to see a dead body they didn't even know was something her mother would make a fuss over. Esther could tell. Esther's mother was always talking about *behavior*. It had to do with not doing things that disturbed others and it went all the way from farting at the dinner table while others were trying to eat to viewing a dead person uninvited.

Tess knew this because she had been around a few times when Esther got chewed out for being somewhere other than where she was supposed to be or coming home an hour later than promised. Tess's mother never worried Tess over behavior. So long as Tess was home by dinner time, in school when everyone else was, and woke up in her own bed, she was free to roam about. The rule was simple: stay out of trouble. There was no fine print. That was a benefit of being one among a small country of eight kids.

Tess was looking at Esther now and Esther could tell Tess was reading her mind even though Esther kept her eyes turned away. Esther got this look on her face—a kicked dog look—whenever she started thinking about what other people would think.

"Dirty," said Tess, "give Esther her nasty bat and let's get going." Tess stood and didn't even bother to brush away the brown bits of grass that clung to her skirt.

Dirty looked from Esther to his sister then back down at the box. Then he set the box on the grass beside Esther and started out after Tess.

"Okay. I'll go," said Esther when Tess and Dirty were almost halfway across the field. The wind was strong and blowing hard across the field now. It was blowing Esther's words right back into her face, and it was in a furious fight with Tess's long red hair.

"I said I'll *go!*" Esther yelled, and she picked up her box and ran to catch them.

A blue car was parked on the street in front of Whitaker-White Funeral Home. It had been parked there for more than an hour and in it, behind the wheel sat a thirty-three year old man who was about to gather up enough of himself to open his car door, go inside and see his dead wife all dressed and laid out in her casket. It was something he knew he wanted to do alone with nobody around to recognize him or feel sorry for him and shake their heads over his terrible, terrible loss, whispering, "The poor man!"

The man, whose name was Raymond Stoner, had been

carrying a strange feeling around with him all morning—from the moment he opened his eyes, fixed his own coffee, read the paper undisturbed and shaved his neck and cheeks and around his beard, being very, very careful to not hurt himself in any way, to when he dressed himself slowly, putting on his underwear and socks and pants and finally a plain white shirt—he had been carrying this feeling of buoyancy, of a lightness of being that led him to a point of near hysteria.

It was due to the knowledge of something. Something he had not even allowed himself to whisper to the empty rooms of his house. It was the knowledge that he was free. A terrible truth after one's wife has died only the day before. But there it was. And even though he could not let this feeling escape him, not through the breathing of air between his lips, not through the quickness of his steps, it was everywhere around him, within and without. She was dead, but he was not. She was dead. *She was dead.* The curtains said so as they moved away from the windows with the breeze. The sunlight said so as it spread out and warmed the kitchen table.

No one had even so much as whispered that he might be visited by such a strange angel of death, and because he was unprepared, it invaded him and his house completely. When he climbed into his car to drive to the funeral home, it climbed in beside him and they drove together with all the windows down, Raymond Stoner and his sweet, free angel and the streets stretched out long and far in all directions and Raymond drove for what seemed hours in circles through his little town before he could remember where he was to go and how he was to get there. And such aimlessness seemed a fine thing, a wonderful thing, a thing he might keep for himself forever if he could just hold on—it must be as simple as holding onto the steering wheel of one's car.

But then he did remember where he was to go and what he was to see and when his car was finally parked outside Whitaker-White Funeral Home, ah!—that is when he knew the simple thing was not holding on to the steering wheel but letting go and that was something he could not do. So he sat in his car for an hour, watching the trees move and waiting for a word or a sign.

That's when Esther and Tess and Dirty came down the street, Esther with the shoe box under one arm, each with a handkerchief out, dabbing their eyes. They were practicing. They would take turns weeping. Esther was the best at putting on a show of emotions. She had been to funerals before whereas the others hadn't, so she could tell Tess and Dirty a thing or two about crying over a dead body. This was no ordinary cry, a few yelps and a sniffle would not do. It had to come from deep down inside, from a person's toes, she told Dirty and Tess, and as this kind of cry was coming up it had to shake a person's whole body. And it helped if you even choked on it a bit, like you were trying to hold in a noisy sneeze.

They practiced shaking and choking and wiping their eyes as the sun warmed the tops of their heads so their hair fairly glowed with the late summer's heat. They could take in the summer in great deep sobbing breaths and blow it back out again and the leaves of the trees which were already beginning to dry would crackle and flash above their heads.

But when they came before the sidewalk at Whitaker-White's, they all three stopped cold and stood at the end of the sidewalk and wondered what it was that suddenly made them have to think about every breath they took in and out of their little bodies.

Dirty was the one to say something first, after they had been standing without a word or any motion for more than five minutes. "Well, let's go in," he said. He looked from Esther to Tess. His face was white despite the summer sun and his freckles stood out plainly on his face and Esther knew that he was still just as scared as ever but Dirty, because he was the downtrodden sort, lived like a fatalist which enabled him, sometimes at the most unexpected moments, to open doors and cross thresholds into rooms where others were slow to go.

Raymond Stoner had been watching them since they first came into sight, wondering what could make them cry so on such a hot summer morning. The sight of them blowing their noses into their handkerchiefs made him think that if he could only find the right frame of mind he might be able to do the same thing and feel a little bit better about how his wife had died, diseased and all, to a point where she didn't even know him in the last few weeks. He began to think even though he had never seen them before that he was one of their party, that they were all meeting together to see a Saturday matinee. He would pay his admission, walk through the doors into a darkened theatre with blood red carpet and velvet curtains on the walls and see a good show. Yes, it would be like watching a film, just like that. So he let go of the wheel, and opened the car door, and even felt a bit of excitement as he stepped out onto the pavement and moved up the walk to the door.

Inside the air was cool. There was light colored carpeting on the floor and pale green hallways stretched out in all directions from the door. Straight ahead was a short wide hall with large open doorways on either side. Before each doorway was a small sign with white lettering and a name. On one: Robert Francis Dinkle. On the other: Eugenia Louise Stoner.

A man in a suit appeared at the end of a hallway. "We're here with our grandmother," Tess lied in a whisper, pointing towards the short wide hall as if to say that "granny" had gone on before. She lowered her head, and the man hesitated, then nodded and at last evaporated like a mirage back into his office. "Now we won't be bothered," Tess said.

When Esther first entered the funeral home she thought of bath soaps, small decorator bath soaps in different shapes and colors like the ones her mother kept in a cut glass dish on the bathroom counter, little green shells and pink roses and pale yellow balls that Esther was never allowed to use because once she washed her hands with them they lost their shape. That's what the place smelled of—unused, dusty bath soaps.

And wax. Once Esther had been to a wax museum. Her father took her when she was seven. She could remember being led through some black, heavy curtains into a large cold room where statues of men and women in stiff clothes stood about, or leaned on chairs, or held on to one another. That place smelled of moth balls, but just beneath the smell of moth balls was the smell of old yellowing wax. There were signs every two or three steps saying *do not touch the figures*! but Esther touched one anyway, she touched Queen Victoria's yellow waxy hand and waited for Queen Victoria's disapproving eyes to shift and glare down at her.

"Here she is," Tess whispered, pointing to the sign outside of Eugenia's room. Then they were standing before the woman. There were flowers and chairs lining the walls and she was off in a corner, merely lying there, her head slightly raised by a pale blue satin pillow. Above her on the wall hung a large framed print, the kind a person might hang over a couch. It showed people walking this way and that way over a stone bridge, some carried umbrellas and were hunched over with their coats pulled tight about them as if they were walking against a cold wind.

It was at this point that Esther realized she was still carrying the shoe box with the bat. She had meant to stash it under a bush before she came in, but here she was now with it under her arm and inside she could hear the bat still clawing about. Tess and Dirty were already making their way to get a closer look, so Esther set the box down on the floor by the doorway which seemed somehow the respectful thing to do.

Then she took a good look at the woman lying there. Esther half expected her to look like the men and women in wax. But she wasn't like that at all. Those figures were as stiff as candles in their poses. And she didn't look like the dead people Esther had seen before either. Her uncle and her great-grandmother were both worn out and pasty even before they died. This woman, this Eugenia lay as if she had only just closed her eyes, as if she had just breathed in a slow restful breath and was holding it for a moment to feel the fullness of air in her lungs. With her great-grandmother and uncle, Esther kept expecting them to open up their eyes or move their hands or sneeze or cough or something. But this woman was so perfect in her stillness, so rested, *so right*, that Esther thought if she reached out and touched her hand the woman would not disapprove at all, and though her eyes would not flutter open, because she was too absorbed by the sweetness of her death and it required all of her attention to be so perfectly dead, she might smile slightly.

Or perhaps it was, as Esther shifted to another foot and saw the shadows move just a little on the dead woman's face, that her face was already stretched a bit in the way of a smile. But if there was anything false about this woman, it was only that. Only in her mouth was there anything that said someone had tried too hard to keep her expression pleasant as her lips were being sealed.

The three of them stood all with such amazement, studying, studying her hands, her face, that none of them remembered to cry or shake or put on even the smallest of shows.

"She looks so peaceful," said Dirty and he turned and Esther caught in his expression a sly look that she had never seen before. Esther would think back later and wonder again and again what came over Dirty at just that particular moment. Dirty looked about the room and his eyes stopped near the door and with his long legs in just three or four steps he'd made it across the room and had the shoe box in his hands with the lid off.

"Dirty!" Tell yelled as the bat fluttered crazily about the room, swooping low near their heads and swerving this way and that to miss them. Tess was laughing and then she was pressing her hand over her mouth to keep from being heard, her face as red as her hair.

Esther heard footsteps in the hall. "Someone's coming!" she hissed. And before she could take a step or make a move, Tess and Dirty were out the doorway, stomping and giggling down the hall, and she was face to face with Raymond Stoner who stood in the doorway looking bewildered and in need of sleep and watching with an open mouth as the bat, still a captive, flew sorrowfully about the room.

As Esther might have expected, she felt her head and limbs getting big again, monstrously big.

Esther looked back over at the lady Eugenia, beautiful, dead and lying undisturbed, just as she was before, bothered not by Esther or the bat or the sad, sleepy man standing in the doorway. She took one moment to wish that Dirty had gotten scratched by that miserable little bat and would have to have rabies shots in the stomach for the next three months, then she felt a cry rising up from inside that nearly suffocated her. It was a cry for the pretty dead woman and for herself and for all the twisted, overgrown ugly things inside and out that she was always trying to keep ahold of and hide.

Before she let out any sound, Esther took in her next breath, covering her lips with her fingertips. "I thought I might have known her!" she said as a way of apology to the man, hating herself for lying at that moment in order to escape. She ran from the room, the bat gliding out after her but veering off down an uncharted hallway that likely led to offices in back. Then Esther was out of the building and running down the street without so much as stopping to see if Dirty and Tess might be hiding behind some bushes somewhere.

Raymond Stoner waited for something else to happen but nothing did. Outside, the day was still heating up, and he was left with nothing—nothing to gaze at but his dead wife, who made no apology whatever. Heat was rising in waves from the ground, and it wasn't even noontime yet.

Red Bank, NJ

The father came home from work early. No one heard him come through the door. He was just there, standing in the doorway, saying, What is going on? and looking from one face to the other. What is going on? What are you doing? he kept saying. Not like someone angry but like someone completely lost as if he was thinking, *I have come into the wrong house. This is not my house and these are not my two daughters and who are these other two girls here*?

His older daughter, Eileen, who was thirteen and overweight and supposed to be on a diet, had food spread out across the counter—potato chips and twinkies and a carton of ice cream. Eileen held an extra large spoon in her hand and was eating ice cream in great big spoonfuls right out of the carton. "Oh, Dad!" she said. But that's all she could say because then she was laughing and laughing, helpless from laughter and couldn't stop laughing even when large tears began to roll down her cheeks.

The other daughter, Karinne, who was eleven, with a tiny, perfect body and long lovely hair and large eyes, all of which made her look much older, made her look like a twenty-five year old in a miniature body, was dancing on the couch. She was doing pliés and turns and leaps with exquisite form and humming to herself as she danced.

Robin, who was twenty and back home in Red Bank, New Jersey for the summer from college, stood in the middle of the kitchen, unanchored and wringing her hands. Robin had lovely hands, plump and soft and smooth-skinned and when she was caught doing something, she couldn't keep them still. "Mr. Harris. It's me—Robin. Ah—I used to babysit for you. For Eileen and Karinne. In high school. I mean, when *I* was in high school."

Robin looked over at Grace as if for help. Her face was red and puffy around the eyes, the way it always got when she was stoned. "This is my friend, Grace. She's from *Missouri*." Robin said this with special emphasis, as she had been doing all week, as if being from Missouri was something like being from Mars.

70

But Mr. Harris didn't seem to hear her. He was still blinking his eyes and looking about, as if someone had just turned on a bright light and he was blinded by it. "Why are you eating ice cream?" he said to Eileen. "Karinne, stop dancing on the couch," he said. But she kept dancing and humming. She was humming Mozart, one of the movements they often did warm ups to in master class. She was a prodigy, one of a dozen extraordinary children from around the country selected to dance with the Joffrey Ballet. Since she was nine years old, she'd spent each year away from her family studying ballet and came home only in the summers.

"Well," said Robin, sliding past Mr. Harris and grabbing her purse from the coffee table. "We were just leaving." She stood just behind his shoulder and gave Grace a "let's get the hell out of here" look and made for the door.

This is how Grace came to make her trip to Red Bank, New Jersey: Her wild college friend Robin who was barely above failing out of the small Missouri college they both attended and who spent most of her past semester with various members of the local rugby team and who had an impressive capacity for combining White Russians with pot and not passing out, invited Grace to make the drive back east with her at the end of the year.

Robin would drive her grandmother's car, an enormous white Cadillac with fins and only 25,000 miles on it. It was vintage, a 1956 model, the year both Robin and Grace were born. Robin's grandmother had driven it for twenty years all over the same college town where Robin and Grace went to school. Robin's parents sent her to school there because Grandmother lived nearby and they thought it would be safe and far away from Robin's high school friends and all the alcohol and drugs they were always doing.

Grandmother had never driven it more than ten miles away from her home because if she ventured any farther away than that, she flew. It was the car her husband Cleo had bought for himself just before he died of a massive coronary and left her with piles and piles of money and for twenty years she drove it around town with plastic covering the seats and the carpeting the way Cleo would have done so that it was like new and even smelled new or perhaps the way a new car in 1956 might have smelled. She felt obligated to drive the thing, to put it to use, a kind of mobile memorial to Cleo and her fidelity. Then, last April, on an impulse no one could have anticipated,

Grandmother bought a new Seville with cash, started seeing a retired bank president five hears her junior, and gave Robin her old car.

Robin had to drive the thing home, and she didn't want to go by herself, so she asked Grace to come along. Grace got good grades and was polite and quiet when she wasn't drunk and as Robin told her, "My parents would approve of you. And I need for them to think I have some stabilizing force in my life now that Grandmother's gone off her rocker and can't be trusted. Otherwise, they'll take one look at my grades and they won't let me come back to school."

Grace was not big on visiting other people's houses. It had something to do with seeing too closely how other people chew their food and use their bathrooms and what they look like when they wake up in the morning. But if she rode with Robin she could go to New York, see a play, Rockefeller Center and Central Park, ride the ferry out to see the Statue of Liberty, and eat lobster. She had a list of things she meant to do.

Grace's parents agreed to pay the one way plane ticket back for the educational experience she would gain from visiting the east, so she packed her bags for two weeks, not knowing for certain what was the right thing to wear around east coast people who always seemed so conscious of such things as far as Grace could tell from meeting Robin and other east coasters who went to her college. Her mother gave her a woven basket to take as a gift. It was handmade of oak strips by an old man who lived in a town called Ozark. It was the thing to do—take a gift to your friend's mother who was taking you into her home and feeding you and looking out for you for two weeks and would hopefully treat you very nearly in the manner that she would treat her own children. Later, when Grace handed the basket over to Robin's mother who was sitting on her bed painting her toenails, Grace could see from the mother's expression what she was thinking—*How quaint. How sweet. Just the thing a sweet girl from a small town out there would do.*

So before the sun was up one morning in May, Grace loaded her bags and her little basket in the deep and wide 1956 Cadillac trunk (or turtle as her mother called it, as everyone in her family called it who was born before 1930), climbed in beside Robin who had a stockpile of cigarette packs in a little plastic bin on the floor and hidden beneath the cigarettes a small leather pouch with several carefully rolled joints, and they drove off, slowly at first until they reached the interstate and the city limits and then Robin pushed the speedometer up to eighty as they barreled toward St. Louis and Columbus and Pittsburgh.

Robin had a twelve year old sister named Mari who had
been declared smart by everyone in her family and by most of
her teachers. She was the family hope. She was promising. She
would make something of herself. Robin and her older brother
had already proven that they wouldn't make themselves much
more than what they already were and so the whole family cast
all of their dreams and aspirations and expectations for greatness
on Mari, even Robin who was always saying to Mari—*keep your
grades up and don't get messed up with drugs and don't hang
around with the wrong kind of people.*

When Robin and Grace pulled the finned Cadillac into the
driveway late that night, Mari was waiting for them, watching
through the curtains of her bedroom window. She could see
Robin in the driver's seat, looking the same with her flat face
and her small red mouth and her blond hair. And she could see
Grace, thin and serious-looking, with ordinary brown hair. Mari
studied Grace as she climbed out of the car, her blouse and her
jeans and her shoes, all of which were ordinary too. Robin had
said on the phone that she was bringing home her Missouri
friend from college who made all "A's" and Mari wanted to see
what smart looked like out there in the midwest, if it was the
same as smart in the east or better or worse, but so far, as Grace
pulled her bags from the trunk of the car, Mari couldn't see
anything distinguishing about this Grace from Missouri, except
that even from this distance she seemed uncomfortable with
something, where she was or who she was or something. And she
seemed always to hold a half a frown on her face, as if she were
always thinking, thinking, thinking about everything. Grace held
one bag in each hand by the handles and from a distance it
looked as though the weight of them stretched her long arms
down even longer than they already were. She looked up at the
very window where Mari had the curtains pulled back, and Mari
was certain Grace from Missouri had seen that someone was
watching her from the second story window.

The first few days they slept until nearly noon, then rose
and lay in the sun by the pool behind Robin's house, then they
ate lunch and spent the late afternoon getting ready to go out to
the bars with Robin's friends. Mari was still in school and
Robin's mother was off volunteering. So they had the house for
themselves most of the day. This is what Robin lived for—getting
wasted, recovering, getting wasted again. Grace went along for

the ride. She didn't drink as much as Robin and past a certain point in the evening nobody noticed or cared that Grace was still drinking from the same glass of beer she was served an hour ago. She didn't know why she liked being around Robin, and Robin didn't know why she liked being around Grace. In fact, they never admitted it to one another, but each made the other just a bit uncomfortable at times, Robin with her plump nervous hands and her appetite for drinking and drugs, Grace with her serious, close-mouthed reserve, always thinking and thinking, but never saying all of what was on her mind.

They always went to the same bars in the same order. This was an important ritual. And once inside they would look to see who was there and with whom, searching, searching the familiar and unfamiliar faces for possibilities, excitement, although Grace had no idea what she was searching for and would usually sit wherever Robin left her after introducing her to a clump of red, sweaty faces as Grace from *Missouri*.

On one night Robin introduced Grace to Stan, an old friend from high school who was just a bit pudgy but had a pleasant face with dark thick hair, a beard and soft blue eyes. Grace wondered briefly why, if he was an old friend, Robin could so readily ignore him. But she was concentrating on a marine at the end of the bar, one who had graduated a few years earlier than Robin, one she had dreamed of sleeping with since she was fourteen.

When Robin spied the marine, she turned to Grace and said, "I'll be back," which really meant—you're on your own. She tapped Stan who was sitting two stools over at the bar and said, "Stan, this is Grace from *Missouri*." Grace thought that if Robin said Missouri in just that way one more time, Grace would hit her. Robin took one long drink to finish her beer, then she made her way down to the end of the bar.

"So. You're from Missouri," Stan said. "I've never been there." He was looking Grace over as he spoke. Her eyes, her face, her hair, her shoulders. He was checking her out. Grace watched as his eyes took her in. "I know someone who moved to St. Louis. Andrew Patella. Italian. You know any Patellas from St. Louis?"

Grace shook her head. "I'm from southern Missouri. I don't know many people from St. Louis."

"I've never been out west," Stan said. "You ever been to the Grand Canyon? What's it like?"

"It's amazing," Grace said. She was glad for something to talk about. "You drive and drive and drive over this flat highway

74

surrounded by all this flat desert and then, it's there. The bottom drops out of the earth right before your eyes. And the colors—" she was not doing it justice. She could not describe it the way it should be described. But she kept trying. "Purples and grays and oranges and these strange colors in between—I don't know the names for them, I don't know if there are names for them. Burros ride down the trails. They take you to the very bottom and bring you back out again."

"You ever been to California?" Stan said. "L.A.? Frisco?" He talked of the cities as if they were people he knew on a first name basis.

"I camped in the redwoods once. Huge trees, old and silent and kind of spooky the way they rise up so high and take up all the sunlight for themselves. There's always this whispering going on around you there." She had already had a few beers and that made her face flushed and it made her talk in this half poetic way. But she didn't care what Stan thought. She was glad for the excuse to hear the sound of her own voice. "Just outside of Frisco we saw whales migrating. You can see them from the highway. Highway 101. We pulled over and watched them for hours. And then in San Francisco we went to—"

"Yeah," said Stan with a flatness in his voice that said he was through listening. "I like Philly. Philly's a nice town. They got good Chinese food there. But New York is where it's at." He looked at her and she wasn't sure what he wanted her to say or do then. "New York is where it's at. So, what are you going to do while you're here?" He had taken his eyes away from her now. He was looking through the smoke to someone at the other end of the bar.

She said she wanted to see a Broadway play and go to the race track and maybe ride the ferry and see the Statue of Liberty.

"Yeah?" he said. "That's good. You should do those things while you're here. I've never done those things. I should do them too someday."

Then he was driving her home. He was smoking a cigarette and driving in his Monte Carlo along streets she didn't know. Robin had left with the marine. "Can you take her home?" she said to Stan. She looked at Grace through squinty eyes and Grace knew she could barely see she was so loaded. "Is that okay, Grace? Stan's alright. You can trust him." She laughed a drunken laugh. "Right, Stan?"

"I have to stop at my house for a minute," he said. "It's just

75

a few blocks down." He had his radio on a classic rock station and it was playing the Doors. "People are strange, when you're a stranger," the radio said.

He pulled his car into the driveway of a small, one story house and the garage door rose and he pulled inside. "You want to get out for a minute?" he said. "Let me open the door for you."

Then he was opening the door and taking her hand to help her out. He closed the door behind her and pressed her against the car, pressed his body up against hers and started kissing her.

She could do that well enough. She could go along with that too. Make her lips go soft so that they seemed willing. "I'd like to take you inside," he whispered, "but my grandmother lives with us. She's home right now."

Good, Grace thought. *Good.* I'm glad your old grandmother is home, your traditional old Catholic Italian grandmother. Was he Italian? No, that was his St. Louis friend, Andrew Patella or Patello or something.

He kept kissing her as if he were enjoying himself, as if he wanted to find out once and for all what it was like to kiss a girl from Missouri. He kissed her until she couldn't breathe and finally she said, "I'm getting tired."

"You want me to take you to Robin's house?"

"Yes. Just take me there. I'm tired," she said. "It must be the time zone difference."

When she got in bed, she pulled the covers up tight around her neck. She was glad to be alone and glad to be in the dark. She thought of Robin's little sister Mari. She suspected that Mari was going through her things while she was away. Opening up drawers and taking out her clothes and unfolding them and folding them back but not in quite the same way. Something was always different whenever she returned to her room. She thought of putting her clothes back in her suitcases and locking them up whenever she was out of the room, but she had failed to bring any luggage keys along.

She held herself under the covers, closed her eyes, and went to sleep.

Robin's father came home from his business trip the next day and they bought a couple of lobsters, a large one and a small one to eat for dinner that night. He left before Grace even arrived and so this was the first she had ever seen of him. He was a vice-president for a big corporation that sold first aid and hygiene products. He was always bringing sample products home for his family to test. At school, Robin had a closet full of super absorbent tampons and toothbrushes. He had a flat face and small red lips just like Robin's, and the first thing he did when he got home was fix everybody but Mari a drink and himself a double.

The lobsters were alive and crawling around on the kitchen floor. The large one had only one claw which was enormous, the size of a platter and Robin's father kept digging empty beer cans out of the trash and slipping them into the lobsters claw and watching him crush the cans. "Watch this," he said. He took an ice cube from Robin's drink and tried to slip it into the large claw as the lobster dragged himself around on the kitchen tiles with his tiny legs. The lobster held his claw open for several seconds then suddenly clamped it shut on the father's finger. He yanked his hand away before the lobster had a good grip.

"Damn. Jesus." Robin's father was red-faced and shaking his hand at his side. Then he laughed and looked at his golfing friend and his golfing friend's second wife who had been invited to join them for dinner and were standing in the kitchen drinking doubles too. "The bastard almost took my hand off."

"That's enough," said Robin's mother. Mari was on the floor next to the smaller lobster saying over and over, Oh! isn't he cute!

"I have to put these things in boiling water for God's sake. Mari, don't get attached to them."

Then they were talking about flexibility. Grace wasn't sure how they had gotten to the topic. She was on her third or fourth gin and tonic, third or fourth already, she couldn't remember—her mind was clouded over and from all the drinking she'd been doing all week.

Grace was bent over, touching her nose to her knees in front of the whole circle of people. Mari and Robin and Robin's mother and father and golfing friends. She could remember saying that she was extremely flexible and now here she was proving it in front of everybody with her butt in the air and her stomach doubled over and all that gin draining straight to her brain.

"That's amazing," the golfing buddy kept saying. Grace slowly rose and she could hear the blood roaring in her ears. "Do that again," said the golfing buddy. The golfing buddy's wife did not say anything.

Grace bent over and pressed her nose against her knees being careful to keep her long legs straight. "Amazing," said the golfing buddy. "I could never do that." He had a small smile on his face as he raised his drink to his lips.

Grace teetered a bit, then pulled herself up just in time. If she had held her nose to her knees a moment longer she would have passed out.

Since Grace was a guest of honor she got one of the claws which were underdone and gelatinous. Robin's father kept going on about the lobster's green stuff which was a delicacy and shoveling great spoonfuls of it into his mouth. He was disappointed that the female lobster wasn't carrying any eggs. Grace managed to finish most of her claw. Afterwards she made her way up the stairs to the bathroom and threw up.

There were only two days left of Grace's visit. In two days she would be on a plane flying home. She would arrive at the airport and her mother would pick her up and have a nice meal planned and she would eat and then lie on the couch and read and watch TV until it was time to go to sleep. Her mother would ask about her trip and Grace would talk about the places she went to see without mentioning the bars, how she had a wonderful time and learned a lot.

But first there was a drive into New York with Robin's mother, a Broadway play to see. They went to the matinee and saw *Dracula*. They watched Renfield go mad and eat flies and watched Count Dracula, played by an Italian with a long nose and a strong jaw, seduce Lucy. It was a pleasant, sexy version of Dracula. There was joking and everyone was quite polite and friendly and Grace found herself almost hoping Dracula would get what he wanted he was so loving about his bloodsucking habits. After the play they waited by the back stage door along with a dozen other fans, just for something do to. After a time the woman who played Lucy came out of the door. She was wearing a brown coat and had a scarf over her head. She used her hand as a clasp under her chin to hold the scarf in place. She smiled and walked past everyone and right into Grace and looked Grace right in the eyes pausing as if she thought she somehow knew Grace or expected something from her, or so it seemed to Grace. "I enjoyed your performance," Grace said.

The woman smiled. "Thank you." Then she walked on down the street and into the crowd of people traveling the sidewalk to apartments or restaurants, to lovers or bosses or children awaiting them somewhere in the city.

They drove past the United Nations and drove past Rockefeller Center and briefly got lost in Harlem on streets where blacks lined up against the buildings and sat on porch stoops, talking in the warm air of the spring evening, barely taking notice of the pale, pale faces of Robin and Robin's mother and Grace, and they saw the Statue of Liberty in the distance from a bridge as they finally headed back to New Jersey and Grace was surprised at how green it was against a darkening evening sky.

When they returned, Stan had left a message for Grace. He wanted to take Grace out. They could go to a bar and see a local band play or drive down the coast to Atlantic City to visit some of his friends. At first Grace thought she might say yes. But she thought of his soft body pushed up against hers in his garage with his grandmother somewhere in the house watching reruns of *Gunsmoke* on TV and decided to go to Mari's junior high open house instead.

It was there that Robin met up with thirteen year old Eileen. Wild Eileen who liked to get high and liked especially the idea of getting her old babysitter high and begged and begged Robin to come to her house tomorrow to visit. "Bring your friend," she said. She was standing in the hallway by the girls' gym, her black hair frizzed out all around her head. "She can come too." She laughed and held herself together as if she had been needing to pee for a year and could barely hold it in. "It will be wild! Too much! Come, oh *come!*"

"Shh!" Robin said. "Okay! Okay. For a little while in the afternoon." And after Robin rejoined her family, she kept whispering to Grace, "I can't believe Eileen gets high! I used to *babysit* her."

They went to the junior high assembly and listened to an eighth grade boy that Mari had been in love with all year sing a rock song with piano accompaniment from the choir director. "*Dust in the wind*," he sang. "*All we are is dust in the wind.*"

He sang the words quickly and with ease. Mari let out a sigh when he was finished. Everyone applauded. And Mari gripped Grace's arm. "He was good, wasn't he. Don't you think he was good?"

"Yes." Grace smiled because she knew that's what Mari wanted her to do.

It was like any junior high assembly anywhere. They visited all of Mari's rooms and saw all of her papers. And everybody oohed and aahed over Mari's fine school work, but especially Grace, because Mari kept turning to her again and again asking *what do you think of this? did you know I got the highest grade in the class on this one?*

79

The highlight of the evening was meeting Frances Ford Coppola whose son was in Mari's class. Robin's father introduced him to Grace so Grace would have something to remember about her trip to the open house. He was shorter than Grace. His white shirt and khaki slacks were rumpled. And it looked as though he hadn't shaved in a few days. He bowed slightly to Grace, but did not offer his hand.

Grace did not like the idea of going to Eileen's house from the start. But she was only going to be with Robin one more day. They rode over in Robin's finned Cadillac, Robin smoking a cigarette and steering with one hand. "Why don't you call your mom," Robin was saying. "Ask her if you can stay another week. I want you to stay. Everybody likes you. Mari wants you to stay. You could go out with Stan."

"I don't know." Grace was looking out the window. They were driving on a narrow street with plain houses. They could have been houses in her own neighborhood. They drove past a Dairy Queen where earlier in the week they had brought Robin's basset hound Freida for an ice cream cone. "Freida loves ice cream," Robin had said as she laid a large cone on the sidewalk before the basset hound. "In the summer we bring her here once a week." Freida was licking the ice cream with a great long tongue, spreading half of the ice cream out in a white pool at Grace's feet.

Then they were in a driveway, climbing out of the car and walking down a sidewalk to a house that looked small from the road but spread out down the backside of a long hill. Eileen was at the door before they even had a chance to ring the bell.

"Come in!" she shouted. She leaped up to the couch and from the couch to the chair. "We started without you!" she sang. She handed Robin a rolled joint from where she stood on the chair.

"This is Karinne. My little sister. Remember, Robin? How little she was when you left for college? Jesus," she said, looking at Karinne. "See what living in New York and dancing with fags can do for you?" Karinne was sitting on the floor with headphones on. She was moving her head back and forth to the music. She stood and began a slow dance. She was barefooted and in shorts and Grace watched her legs, small and perfect and muscled. She moved like an older woman who loved the feel of her own muscles and Grace could imagine men forgetting she was a child and falling in love with her, with her muscles and her smallness and her long, smooth brown hair.

80

Robin was talking and smoking and laughing and every once in a while she would pass the cigarette to Grace and Grace would smoke it a bit and tell herself that this would be over soon enough and she would be on a plane going home. Eileen was bouncing from the chair to the couch and back and Karinne had the headphones off now and was humming Mozart. She had gone from free form dancing to leaps and pirouettes. And Grace was feeling sick again, not the kind of sick that came from drinking gin and tonic and practically standing on her head and eating undercooked lobster.

This was a different kind of sickness, the nausea of knowing for the first time who she was, this Grace from Missouri who ate from her friend's table and slept in her friend's bed and had believed all along what every one else seemed to believe, that she was a nice girl.

Karinne was a beautiful child dancer with her long brown hair curled at the ends and her small breasts and her arms making great circles through the room. It was the first time Grace had ever seen someone so young dance such a dance, leaping from chair to chair as she did. It was strange and haunting, right and awful at once. Karinne was moving faster and faster about the room. She was dancing so fast that she made Grace dizzy with her movement, and Grace rose suddenly and began chasing after the girl, not because she wanted to join in but because she wanted to take hold of the child and make her stop. Grace grabbed for the girl more than once in the chase, but Karinne kept dancing just beyond her grasp.

Robin and Eileen had moved into the kitchen and Eileen was talking about her mother who had left them two years ago and moved to California. The Bitch, Eileen called her. "The Bitch wants me to come out for a month this summer," she was saying. She was practically crying and tearing through the freezer for ice cream. "But I told Daddy I wasn't going."

She had the ice cream on the counter and was digging into it with a large spoon and that's when the father came through the door.

"What is going on? What is going on? What are you doing?" he kept saying. He was pleading with them. "Why are you eating that ice cream? *Karinne, stop dancing on the couch!*"

All evening and the next morning Grace was waiting for the police to show up and arrest Robin and Grace for contributing to the delinquency of minors at least, but no one came and when they were finally in the airport and Grace had checked her luggage and gotten her boarding pass, she felt as though she was about to make a narrow escape.

The whole family had come along to say goodbye except for Father who left the night before on another business trip. Before he left he went through the family closet and pulled out all the sample products he could find to give to Grace so that she could take them home. Dozens of toothbrushes, and bottles of skin softening lotion, and first aid kits in plastic boxes with tape and safety pins and bandages and little first aid booklets that explained how to make a tourniquet and what to do in case of electrocution.

Robin's mother took them to the V.I.P. lounge where she bought Grace one last drink. Then a woman's voice was calling for boarders on Grace's plane. Robin's mother and Robin and Mari all watched as Grace walked through the gate.

She turned her back on them and headed down the tunnel. "What a *nice* girl," Robin's mother was saying. A few more minutes passed and then, Grace was blasting out of New Jersey and hurtling back home at four hundred miles per hour.

Rats

I

By the light of her back porch, Elizabeth wrapped the rope around the entire length of the trap cage and drew the ends into a tight hard knot. She was careful as she did this to rattle the cage as little as possible, but the rat inside was still disturbed. It would sit quietly for a moment, then suddenly turn and scream a terrible high-pitched scream that made Elizabeth's fingers shake as she worked to secure the doors of the cage with the rope.

It was a Norwegian rat—a species that lived off of human refuse. It was grey with a long bristly tail that at its base was as thick as Elizabeth's thumb. It had black round eyes the size of expensive pearls and as shiny as black pearls too—eyes, it seemed to Elizabeth, that read her every move and knew her intentions.

When Elizabeth was certain the doors of the trap could not open, she lifted the cage by the handle and carried it to a large metal wash tub filled with water. Then she lowered the cage into the water until it was completely submerged.

Immediately the rat rose to the top of the cage. It moved with surprising agility beneath the water, with the frantic gracefulness of one trying to survive. The rat clawed at the cage, paused almost thoughtfully, then lunged at the top of the cage once more, scratching and biting the wire mesh. Finally, it slackened, quivered, and sank to the bottom. Elizabeth watched for several seconds, surprised at how quickly the rat had drowned, and when she was certain the rat was dead, she lifted the cage from the water, loosened the rope, and as best she could, deposited the rat into a plastic bag which she dropped into the trash.

And at last, after washing her hands several times, she went back to bed.

It was after three in the morning when she awoke again. She heard a noise, the sound of someone opening a gate. Sometimes she would dream that a thief was creeping through her house, a faceless man who wanted to take something from her, and she would hear the sound of his footsteps, the sound of his breathing like sand paper drawn back and forth over wood, and awaken with her heart beating loud in her ears. But this sound was not a part of a dream, because now, with her eyes wide open she heard the gate close.

She rose and pulled on a loose sweatshirt and sweat pants, listening all the while for another sound. She walked down the hallway, the floor creaking beneath her feet. It was a wooden floor, old, and it made noise with every step. When Elizabeth first moved into the sixty year old home, she was not used to a house that talked as much as this one. If she so much as shifted her weight from one foot to another the floor let her know about it. Now, as she walked down the hall, the floor told anyone who cared to listen where she was going.

She reached the back door and pulling open the curtain, looked out the window. There she saw a thin man with grey hair standing over the tub where she had hours earlier drowned her first rat. It was Jack, her neighbor. They had agreed to keep Elizabeth's tub full of water and use it to drown rats whenever needed. It was Elizabeth's idea. She wanted to have someone to cooperate with on such a grisly task. She was glad to see Jack now that she was awake so early in the morning.

This rat business was keeping her up most nights. Nobody said anything about a rat problem when she signed the contract to buy the house, not the realtor or the owner or the neighbors across the street. She found out about it nearly a month later when, as she was sunning her her small back yard, a rat the size of a summer sausage ran across her blanket and disappeared under a stack of wood behind Jack's garage. It even paused at one point and turned back as if to study Elizabeth before it went on its way.

She opened the door and stepped out onto the porch. "What kind of soup you got cookin' there?" she said. When she talked to Jack, her voice always sounded more cheerful than she was. It took on a neighborly drawl that almost embarrassed her. Now, as dark and still as it was, her voice almost echoed.

Jack turned to look at Elizabeth and laughed. He shook his head. "I heard the trap close right under my bedroom window."

He looked back at the water in the tub. "This old guy was squealing and making such a racket that I couldn't sleep."

Elizabeth stepped over next to Jack but avoided looking into the water. "I know," she said. "I hear them squeaking and rattling around too."

These were supposed to be humane traps. A woman from the city health department brought them by the day after Elizabeth called and told them about her rat friend. The trap had a door at either end and a tray inside where the bait was set. When the rat stepped up on the tray, the trap doors closed.

The health department wanted the first few rats while they were still alive to test them for diseases. The woman who brought the traps told Elizabeth to call when she caught a rat and she would come pick it up. Elizabeth felt sorry for the Health Department woman. Her name was Brenda and she was just out of college and this was her first job. She was a biology major or some such thing. Elizabeth was sure that none of her college classes had taught her how to look a wild rat in the eye and kill it.

When Brenda brought the traps out on the first day she looked uncomfortable and in a hurry to get away. She kept glancing around the yard as she talked. And when she explained to Elizabeth how to bait and set the trap, Elizabeth noticed Brenda's hands were shaking.

"I guess this has been going on for years." Brenda had said, after she set a trap for Elizabeth and placed it by the garage. "When we got your phone call, somebody in the office said, 'Oh, no! Not Linden Court again!'" Brenda laughed and avoided looking at Elizabeth.

"It's the woman down at the end of the street," Brenda said, as she began walking back to her truck. "She's got all those dogs and she puts out all kinds of food for the birds and squirrels. Bread crusts and stuff." Brenda was wearing a khaki shirt and pants and brown boots. The uniform made her look heavier than she probably was. She was a pretty girl, with thick black hair and pale skin and freckles. Maybe she was in a sorority in college, one of the more down to earth sororities. And now she was catching rats. Elizabeth wondered how long she would last at this job. "I told that woman she had to clean up her yard, get her wood up off the ground," Brenda said. She climbed into her truck and was suddenly cheerful, glad to be leaving. "We've already had her in court once over this." She started her truck and waved at Elizabeth. "Good luck!" she said, as she backed down Elizabeth's drive.

Now, Brenda was probably sound asleep in a new apartment somewhere on the edge of the city where rats were not yet a problem.

Elizabeth crossed her arms over her chest, not because she was cold, standing on her porch next to Jack, waiting for another rat to drown. But because she was feeling bad inside—bad about buying an old house in an old neighborhood because the trees were large and beautiful, bad about having rats in her back yard and being newly divorced. Elizabeth glanced at Jack. He was staring down at the water and the rat long since drowned. Neither of them spoke. Elizabeth watched Jack for a long time before Jack finally looked up and smiled.

"Well, he said, "I guess I better do something with this old fellow." He waited, as if he knew she didn't want to watch what he was about to do.

"Good night, Jack," she said.

"Good night."

With that, she went back inside and lay in bed with her eyes closed wishing hard that she could get back to sleep.

III

Mrs. Anne Farble had taken to shooting her rats with a pistol. Mrs. Farble was the woman at the end of the street, the one who was responsible for all the rat problems in the first place. She didn't have time to mess with traps. If a rat passed by as she sat on her porch in the late evening reading the newspaper, she'd take up her pistol and usually get it in one shot. The rats never got much farther than the dog water dish.

People in the neighborhood heard Mrs. Farble's gun go off as darkness fell. But they assumed it was a car backfiring or firecrackers.

She didn't worry much about disposing of the carcasses either. She just flipped them over her fence into the back yard of an apartment complex behind her property. On a windy day three or four dead rats could smell pretty sour, but Mrs. Farble never did have a sensitive nose.

She lived alone in her small two bedroom house. Her yard was completely fenced in front and back, and over the years she had nailed up old doors and pieces of plywood and scraps of lumber to her fence so that she had fashioned a wall of privacy. Inside the fence she let her shrubs grow up high against the walls of her house. She kept her small front lawn trimmed and through the spring and summer tended a few petunias and tiger lilies and snap dragons. But the back yard was merely a pallet of hard brown dirt where the dogs had worn the grass down to a few green sprigs now and again popping up through the cracks. Mrs. Farble had built a trough where she scattered grain and breadcrumbs for squirrels and birds and even her dogs to feed.

Squirrels from all over the neighborhood would travel down the telephone wires to Mrs. Farble's back yard. Often a fight would erupt between two squirrels or two cardinals or even a squirrel and a jay who were both going after the same crust of bread. Sometimes people several houses down from Mrs. Farble would find bits of bread or an orange rind in their yard, left there by a squirrel too full to finish, or dropped by a bird on her way back to the nest.

The rats were most polite. They waited until nightfall to emerge from the honeycomb of rat holes that ran beneath the dog houses and stretched under the neighbors' back yards. The males were as large as young cats, though with their short legs and claw-like feet and their way of half hopping half walking across the dirt they didn't look like cats at all.

IV

Elizabeth had caught her second rat. Elizabeth figured that having drowned one rat, the next would be easier. But when she checked her trap the very next night and saw a second rat inside she felt no less mortified at having to do something with that rat as well. In fact, she left the animal there in his cage all day while she went to work. And when she got home and made herself look out the back window, she saw that the rat was still there. It had been raining since noon. The rat had pushed himself up against one side of the cage and sat hunched and motionless. On occasion it raised its head and squeaked and Elizabeth felt as if she'd been cruel to leave it for so long. Even so, she couldn't bring herself to go out and pick up the cage by the handle with the rat inside and tie the door up again and drown it. Once she moved the rat, it would become agitated and start banging about the cage like the one before.

She couldn't call Ben, her ex-husband, and ask him to kill it for her. He would spend a large part of the time telling her how unwise it was to buy a house in an old neighborhood in the first place. And he would want to look around the house, see how she was living without him. He was the fussy one, about the way the house was kept, about keeping clutter to a minimum. It still astounded Elizabeth to think that he left her. He met a divorced woman with two children while he was taking night classes at the local college. "She seems to know what she wants out of life," her ex-husband had said of this woman when he was trying to explain to Elizabeth why he was leaving. If Elizabeth asked him to come over and help her kill a rat, he would tell her how unsanitary it was to have rats in her yard. And then, Elizabeth imagined, he would go home and tell his wife about it.

Elizabeth couldn't ask her mother to help either. Her mother lived across town in a large house by herself. It was the house where Elizabeth grew up and the house where her father died. If she told her mother about the rats, her mother would call every day and ask about "her situation." She would call Elizabeth and say, "Well, how is your situation today?" As if Elizabeth had gotten pregnant out of wedlock, and her mother was doing her best to be supportive about it.

So she asked Jack to help her. She went over to his house and knocked on the front door. When he answered he had a cookie in his hand and he smiled at her and said, "Come in!" Lois, he said, was at work. She was a nurse and worked the three to eleven shift. Jack was a mechanic. "I was just having my desert," Jack said. "Want a cookie?"

Without waiting for her to answer he walked back to his kitchen and emerged with one wrapped in a napkin. He handed it to her. "Sit down!" he said, and he cleared away the evening paper which was scattered across the couch.

Jack collected clocks and there were at least twenty-five of various shapes and sizes placed about the room, all of them ticking. Elizabeth had been there once on the hour when they all went off, their chimes ringing with a comic urgency, some quick and light, others solemn as if to celebrate or warn of the passing of another hour. He ran one cuckoo clock slow, so that it would be the final solitary sounding of the hour.

Jack was going about the room, picking things up and putting them away. "I talked to Mrs. Farble today," he said. He smiled as he pushed his slippers beneath a chair. Elizabeth noticed as he moved how graceful he was, thin and strong for a man over sixty. "I hope I'm not repeating stories, but I was working outside, cleaning out some of the brush by her fence—you know, because of the rats—and Mrs. Farble came out of her house and yelled at me. 'Have you got rocks in your head?' she says. Because it was middle of the day and hot. Well, she's always running men down, you know, so I says," Jack laughed, "I told her, 'Well somebody's got to do it. You know how women are, they might do something once, but then that's it.'" Jack straightened and watched Elizabeth from the corner of his eye. "She looked at me and said, 'Oh, horseshit.'"

Jack laughed again and Elizabeth laughed with him. She had never met Mrs. Farble, but Jack told her enough stories that Elizabeth had an idea of what she was like.

"I got this for my trouble though." Jack raised his arm to reveal large blisters from his fingers to his elbow. "Poison Ivy. It gets in my blood and makes me feel feverish. I tried to be careful," he said.

The poison ivy looked terrible, and Elizabeth felt the kind of queasy burning that she always felt when she saw someone sick or hurt in some way. She told Jack she was sorry about his poison ivy. And then they were silent for several seconds, Elizabeth on the couch and Jack by the television, neither one looking at the other until at last Elizabeth realized that Jack was waiting for her to tell him what she came for.

It surprised her how difficult it was to ask. She was embarrassed, didn't want to seem nervous or bothered, but even so when she finally began to get the words out, her voice was halting. "I've caught another—rat. And I was wondering, Could you—help me with it?"

Without hesitation, Jack said, "Sure," as if the request were remarkable for its simplicity. He led Elizabeth through the kitchen to the back door. As they were passing through, Elizabeth noticed his dinner plates neatly stacked in the sink. "I've got some rope in my garage," he said. They stepped out the back door, and Jack disappeared into his garage, emerging moments later with a rope in hand. "Where is it? By the garage?" he said. He walked around the corner of his own garage and stepped into Elizabeth's yard. "This'll just take a minute," he said. Elizabeth half expected him to follow with, "And it won't hurt a bit."

She stood on her own porch and waited. She could hear the rat squeaking and Jack was talking to it in an odd way, trying to calm it with his voice, saying "there, there" and "shh!" as if it were a child. He brought the rat around the corner, holding the cage by its handle. Elizabeth felt she should be there somehow. She felt ridiculous and awful about the whole business, and somehow she thought it might improve her character if she stood by Jack when the deed was done.

Jack lowered the rat into the tub as they had done before. As agreed, Elizabeth kept the tub full of water. But she changed the water each time a rat was drowned, as if in some absurd way each rat deserved to die in his own fresh water.

Jack turned to Elizabeth and said, "You know, I haven't checked my trap. Come on," he said. "Lois wants you to pick some of her flowers. They need to be thinned."

It was kind of him to find an excuse like that and Elizabeth followed him into his yard. The day was beginning to soften into a mild darkness. Lois's garden extended the full length of her back yard and now in the darkened air, lightning bugs hovered over the flowers. Lois kept all kinds of flowers in her garden and mixed them all together so that the whole garden looked like a pleasing accident. Elizabeth was about to break a flower she couldn't name from its stem, when Jack called to her. He was in the far corner of the yard, by Mrs. Farble's fence, kneeling on the ground. "Look what I caught," he said, as Elizabeth approached him.

Inside the trap was a cardinal, brilliant red with a defiant yellow mark above its beak. Like the rats, it would rest quietly for a moment then suddenly beat against the cage and cry. "How did you get in there?" Jack said to the bird.

On the other side of the fence, Mrs. Farble was sitting on her porch. She hadn't seen many rats in the last few days. Several had been caught in traps or shot and there were fewer of them to venture out. Most of those caught had been females who were foraging for their young. And deep inside the holes, tiny rats waited, hungry. But just now, by the fence she saw a movement and she raised her pistol and fired.

In a few years, Mrs. Farble would kill Jack in this way. The rats would die off for a year or two, then come back strong. One spring evening as Elizabeth was eating dinner she would look out her kitchen window to see one hopping across her front lawn. Mrs. Farble's eyesight would fail and while Jack was kneeling in the garden pulling up weeds, Mrs. Farble would put a bullet through his head.

But this time, the bullet lodged in the dirt on her side of the fence just at the moment that Jack let the cardinal go free. Elizabeth and Jack had jumped at the sound of the gun. And now, they all watched, Elizabeth, Jack, and Mrs. Farble, as the bird rose above the fence, almost purple with the darkness, and disappeared into the night.

A Woman, Two Fools and the Slave

Once there was a woman with very big teeth—teeth so big her mouth could not contain them, and so they stuck out from between her lips. These teeth were a source of great grief for her. They made her feel as though her whole body, her whole spirit was as large and stupid as her great big teeth.

"Oh, God!" she cried out one day, holding her hands up to the sky. "God! Why such big teeth?" She waited, her teeth turned up to the heavens, and when no answer came, she turned away and went to lie under a tree.

At this time, a boy leading an ox and cart came slowly down the road.

He said to the woman, "Woman, why are you lying beneath that tree?"

And the woman answered him, "My teeth are big, and my spirit is heavy. I will lie here until the grass has grown up through my eye sockets, until mushrooms spring up from my knuckles."

The boy was so moved by her words he could go no further. So he left his ox and cart by the road and went to lie down beside her.

Just then, a goatherd came down the road. He led a herd of six or seven goats, each with a small bell about its neck. Each bell struck a different tone as the goats trotted along bleating and snorting to blow the dust from their noses.

The goatherd was singing a ballad about a good widow and the widow's three sons, but when he saw the boy and the woman, he stopped.

He said to the boy, "Boy, why are you lying beneath that tree?"

And the boy answered him, saying, "This woman's teeth are big and her spirit is heavy. She is going to lie beneath this tree until the grass grows up through her eye sockets, until mushrooms spring from her knuckles."

The goatherd was so deeply moved by the boy's words he

could go no further. So he left his goats and went to lie down beside the boy and the woman, his eyes wet with sorrow.

Seven years passed and no one came or went. The great ox had long since pulled its cart off in search of a hard-hearted boy who would not lay down his life beside the first grief-stricken, buck-toothed woman he met.

The goats too had wandered away, but not without waiting a full two years for the goatherd to come to his senses. They stood over him and jingled their bells. They stomped at the dust, their hooves like mallets beating the dull drum of the earth. They whispered among themselves and breathed stale goat's breath over him. But the goatherd did not budge.

Once the goats were gone, the only motion beneath the tree was that of grass shooting up like needles. The only sound: a soft and terrible popping as mushrooms burst through the skin of the earth.

At last, there appeared on the road a slave. On his back he carried a large sack of grain for market, the weight of which was so great he staggered like a drunk as he walked. With each step the weight of the sack grew greater so that by the time he was near the tree, he careened from one side of the road to the other, running to keep ahead of his sack until he tripped and fell on his face.

The slave sat up and spat. He blinked and stood to brush the dust from his shirt. Then with two hands and all of his strength, he pulled the sack into the shade of the tree.

"Ah, me," he said, as he sat on the grass.

He plucked a blade of grass and held it beneath his nose to be sure he was breathing, and when the blade twitched with the wind of his nostrils, he could not tell whether to laugh or cry.

Night was beginning to fall. He found the woman's two big teeth and struck them together until he had a fire.

He washed his hands in the goatherd's tears, and picked mushrooms—white and firm as a young boy's knuckles.

And when he had roasted each mushroom and eaten them all, chewing slowly and with care the way any slave would who knows that nothing in life is given or received without great cost, he spread himself beneath the tree, beneath the stars, and listened as crickets wept throughout the night.